Stories on the page are so beautifully neat. All that lovely black print; those lovely straight lines and paragraphs and pages. But stories are living things, creatures that move and grow in the imaginations of writer and reader. They must be solid and touchable just like the land, and must have fluid half-known depths just like the sea. These stories take place in a real world—the streets in which I grew, the fields and beaches over which I walked. People I know appear in them. But in fiction, real worlds merge with dreamed worlds. Real people walk with ghosts and figments. Earthly truth goes hand in hand with watery lies.

David Almond

half a creature
from the
sea

half a creature from the sea

A Life in Stories

DAVID ALMOND

illustrated by Eleanor Taylor

CANDLEWICK PRESS

Introduction and story introductions © 2014 by David Almond

"Slog's Dad" copyright © 2006 by David Almond
(First published in *So, What Kept You?*)

"May Malone" copyright © 2008 by David Almond
(First published in *The Children's Hours*)

"When God Came to Cathleen's Garden"
copyright © 2009, 2010 by David Almond
(First published in *Sideshow: Ten Original Tales of Freaks,
Illusionists, and Other Matters Odd and Magical*)

"The Missing Link" copyright © 2008, 2014 by David Almond
(First published in *The Times*)

"Harry Miller's Run" copyright © 2008 by David Almond
(First published in conjunction with Great North Run Culture)

"Half a Creature from the Sea" copyright © 2007 by David Almond
(First published in *Click*)

"Joe Quinn's Poltergeist" copyright © 2014 by David Almond

"Klaus Vogel and the Bad Lads" copyright © 2009 by David Almond
(First published in *Free? Stories About Human Rights*)

Illustrations copyright © 2014 by Eleanor Taylor

First U.S. edition 2015

Library of Congress Catalog Card Number 2015931431
ISBN 978-0-7636-7877-7

15 16 17 18 19 20 BVG 10 9 8 7 6 5 4 3 2 1

Printed in Berryville, VA, U.S.A.

This book was typeset in Skia.
The illustrations were done in mixed media.

Candlewick Press
99 Dover Street
Somerville, Massachusetts 02144

visit us at www.candlewick.com

For Tim and Rachel

CONTENTS

Introduction 1

Slog's dad 15

May Malone 35

when God came to Cathleen's garden 53

the missing link 77

Harry Miller's run 99

half a creature from the sea 133

Joe Quinn's poltergeist 163

Klaus Vogel & the bad lads 203

I'll

start

with

things I can hardly

remember,

things I've

been told about,

things that are like

fragments of a dream.

I grew up in a town called Felling-on-Tyne. My first home was an upstairs flat in White's Buildings, a cluster of houses at the edge of the town's main square. It had high white walls and wide dark doors, and a tiny kitchen where the sink perched on a timber frame. The tin bath hung on the kitchen wall. Steep, crumbling steps led to a small backyard and the outside toilet. My mother used to say that before she opened the door to any room, she'd tap on it to make sure the mice scattered to their holes in the skirting boards and floors. There were hundreds of them, she told me. Thousands! I remember the smell of damp, of the outside loo. Dust cascaded through the shafts of light that poured through the narrow kitchen windows. Dead flies clustered on dangling flypapers. Sirens blared from the factories by the river, foghorns hooted from the distant sea. There were four of us then: Mam; Dad; my brother, Colin; and me.

Mam said that I was just a few months old when she first took me to visit my Uncle Amos. She'd wheel me in my pushchair through the square, past the Jubilee pub, Dragone's coffeehouse, Myers' pork shop. Down onto the steep, curving High Street, lined with a butcher's, grocer's, tailor's, pubs. A pink pig's head would be grinning out from Myers' window. There'd be boxes of bright fruit stacked outside Bamling's. A great codfish, bigger than a boy, would lie on the marble slab outside the fishmonger's. You could smell the fish and chips from Fosters', the beer from the open windows of the Halfway House, oil and rust from Howie's cluttered junkyard behind its swinging stable door. We'd pass by the cracked pale faces and legs of the mannequins of Shepherd's department store. All the way, Mam'd be calling out greetings to family and neighbors. They'd be leaning down to grin and coo at me, maybe to slip a coin into my little hand. Always, above the rooftops, the thin steeple of our church, St. Patrick's, pointed to the blue.

Halfway down the street, my mother would turn into a narrow alleyway and carry me into Amos's printing shop. There'd been a few generations of printers in our family, and Amos was the latest. He printed the local newspaper in that dark small place, on a pair of ancient printing machines. Do

I remember it? I like to think I do, but I guess I only really remember my mother's words. She told a tale that one day when she was in there, with me lying in her arms, Amos pulled a lever, and the printing machines began to clatter and turn, and the pages of the newspaper began to stream out from them, and I started to wriggle and jump in her arms, and to point and giggle at the pages. Just as a baby's eyes are caught by flashing lights or flying birds, my eyes were caught by print — and I'd be in love with it for evermore. Maybe I began to be a writer that day in that little printing shop, a time I can't remember, when I was a few months old.

Amos was a writer as well as a printer. He wrote poems, stories, novels, plays. At family parties, after a couple of drinks, he'd take a piece of paper from his pocket and read a poem to us. Some would roll their eyes and giggle, but I loved him for it. I had an uncle who was a writer; I could be the same. None of his work was ever published or performed, but it didn't matter to him. He kept on writing for the love of it, and for his family and friends. I was just a boy when I told him shyly of my own ambitions. "Yes," he said, "do that!" He also told me, "Don't let your writing separate you from the people and places that you love."

White's Buildings was eventually classified as a slum and was demolished. We moved to a brand-new council estate, The Grange, beside the brand-new bypass on the eastern edge of town. I went to St. John's Catholic primary school, a somber stone-built establishment next to the river. Amos closed the printing shop and moved away, but the sign above the alleyway remained for years:

ALMOND
PRINTER

I passed beneath it a thousand times as I continued to grow.

I played with my friends on the fields above the town. I roamed farther, to the hills beyond the fields, where there were abandoned coal mines and spoil heaps, tussocky paddocks with ponies in them, newt ponds, ruined stables. From up there, you could see the whole town sloping away: the streets leading to the square, the factories below that, the river lined with shipyards, the city of

Newcastle with its bridges and towers and steeples. To the north, the distant bulges of the Cheviots in a haze. To the west, the hills of County Durham, the pitheads and winding gear of the coal mines. To the south, more fields, lanes, hawthorn hedges, then Sunderland, then the towns of Teesside on the far horizon. To the east, the dark North Sea. It seemed that much of the world, in all its variety, was visible from this little place.

I started to scribble stories of my own. I read books from the local library. I dreamed of coming back to this library one day in the future, to find books with my own name on them standing on the shelves. Once or twice I dared to admit to others that I wanted to be a writer. I remember one day getting the response, "But you're just an ordinary kid. And you come from ordinary little Felling. What on earth will you write about?"

As time has gone on, I've found myself writing more and more about that little place. Many of my stories spring from it. They use its landscape, its language, its people, and turn it into fiction — half imaginary, half real. The stories in this book are all in some way connected to that "ordinary" place. I try to do what many writers have done before me: show that ordinary places can be extraordinary.

T he story of "Slog's Dad" takes place right in the heart of the town, in Felling Square. This was a small, low-walled area with an ancient fountain and water trough at the center. There were benches where folk sat to while away the day, to take a rest after walking up the steep High Street, or to sit and wait for the Black Bull or the Jubilee to open. On one side of the square was Ray Lough's barber's, with its plate-glass window, its short line of chairs. Ray would have no truck with modern styles. Boys might go in asking for a James Dean or a Beatles cut but they'd all get the same: short back and sides finished with lotion slapped on; the kind that set hard as soon as it hit the open air. Just next door was my grandfather's betting shop. The name in the window — John Foster Barber — caused some men to walk in for a haircut, but instead they'd find my grandfather puffing on his pipe behind the counter, men standing around earnestly reading *Sporting Life,* and crackly radio reports of horse race results coming from speakers on the walls. The square, and the High Street, and many of the shops and pubs still exist. Not Lough's, and not the betting shop. My Uncle Maurice took it over when my grandfather retired, but then Ladbrokes opened in the square and Maurice moved the shop to Hebburn, a few miles away, to catch the custom of shipyard workers. But shipbuilding declined, then quickly crashed, and the betting shop was one of the many businesses that went down with it.

Myers' pork shop sold the best pork pies, the best pork sandwiches, and the best saveloy dips in the area. Saveloys are a kind of sausage. They seemed to my friends and me to be the height of deliciousness, especially inside a soft bread roll with stuffing, onions, and mustard and dipped into a shallow tray of Myers' special gravy. A saveloy dip with everything: a taste of Heaven!

I was a Catholic, like many of my friends. We were taught to believe that when good people died, they went to be with God. (The bad, of course, went to

Hell to burn for all eternity.) Sometimes, when the sun shone down and the sky was blue and the river glittered far below, the larks singing over the high fields, Heaven didn't seem too far away. We were constantly reminded of its inhabitants, too. There were statues of Jesus and his mother, and of saints and angels in St. Patrick's. We all had prayer books and rosary beads and little statues and pictures in our homes.

Cheery priests were familiar figures in the streets — off to visit the sick, to comfort the bereaved, or to have a glass of whiskey with a parishioner. Tramps were often seen too. There was one in particular who lived, it was said, somewhere in the hills above town. No one knew his name, or where he'd come from. He was a silent, swiftly walking man with flaxen hair. He seemed at ease, untroubled by the world, and he was a romantic figure to boys like me. To live a life of freedom in the open air! Who wouldn't desire such a life? Sometimes I'd see him sitting alone on a bench in the square, just as Slog's dad does in the story. I longed to try to talk to him, but I never did.

This story came from a fragment from the

notebook of the great short-story writer Raymond Carver, which I used as an inspiration for a tale of my own. One line jumped out at me: "I've got how much longer?" As soon as I wrote it down in my own notebook, "Slog's Dad" sprang to life. I switched on the computer, began to write. There was a boy called Davie, walking across the square with his friend Slog. There was a bloke on the bench. There was Myers' pork shop with its delicious saveloys. . . .

Slog's dad

Spring had come. I'd been running around all day
with Slog and we were starving. We were crossing the
square to Myers' pork shop. Slog stopped dead in his
tracks.

"What's up?" I said.

He nodded across the square.

"Look," he said.

"Look at what?"

"It's me dad," he whispered.

"Your dad?"

"Aye."

I just looked at him.

"That bloke there," he said.

"What bloke where?"

"Him on the bench. Him with the cap on. Him with the stick."

I shielded my eyes from the sun with my hand and tried to see. The bloke had his hands resting on the top of the stick. He had his chin resting on his hands. His hair was long and tangled and his clothes were tattered and worn, like he was poor or like he'd been on a long journey. His face was in the shadow of the brim of his cap, but you could see that he was smiling.

"Slogger, man," I said. "Your dad's dead."

"I know that, Davie. But it's him. He's come back again, like he said he would. In the spring."

He raised his arm and waved.

"Dad!" he shouted. "Dad!"

The bloke waved back.

"See?" said Slog. "Howay."

He tugged my arm.

"No," I whispered. "No!"

And I yanked myself free and I went into Myers', and Slog ran across the square to his dad.

★　　★　　★

Slog's dad had been a binman, a skinny bloke with a creased face and a greasy flat cap. He was always puffing on a Woodbine. He hung on to the back of the bin wagon as it lurched through the neighborhood, jumped off and on, slung the bins over his shoulder, tipped the muck into the back. He was forever singing hymns—"Faith of Our Fathers," "Hail Glorious Saint Patrick," stuff like that.

"Here he comes again," my mam would say as he bashed the bins and belted out "O Sacred Heart" at eight o'clock on a Thursday morning.

But she'd be smiling, because everybody liked Slog's dad, Joe Mickley, a daft and canny soul.

First sign of his illness was just a bit of a limp; then Slog came to school one day and said, "Me dad's got a black spot on his big toenail."

"Just like *Treasure Island*, eh?" I said.

"What's it mean?" he said.

I was going to say death and doom, but I said, "He could try asking the doctor."

"He has asked the doctor."

Slog looked down. I could smell his dad on him, the scent of rotten rubbish that was always on him. They lived just down the street from us, and the whole house

17

had that smell in it, no matter how much Mrs. Mickley washed and scrubbed. Slog's dad knew it. He said it was the smell of the earth. He said there'd be nowt like it in Heaven.

"The doctor said it's nowt," Slog said. "But he's staying in bed today, and he's going to hospital tomorrow. What's it mean, Davie?"

"How should I know?" I said.

I shrugged.

"It's just a spot, man, Slog!" I said.

Everything happened fast after that. They took the big toe off, then the foot, then the leg to halfway up the thigh. Slog said his mother reckoned his dad had caught some germs from the bins. My mother said it was all the Woodbines he puffed. Whatever it was, it seemed they stopped it. They fitted a tin leg on him and sent him home. It was the end of the bins, of course.

He took to sitting on the little garden wall outside the house. Mrs. Mickley often sat with him and they'd be smelling their roses and nattering and smiling and swigging tea and puffing Woodbines. He used to show off his new leg to passersby.

"I'll get the old one back when I'm in Heaven," he said.

If anybody asked was he looking for work, he'd laugh.

"Work? I can hardly bliddy walk."

And he'd start in on "Faith of Our Fathers" and everybody'd smile.

Then he got a black spot on his other big toenail, and they took him away again, and they started chopping at his other leg, and Slog said it was like living in a horror picture.

When Slog's dad came home next, he spent his days parked in a wheelchair in his garden. He didn't bother with tin legs: just pajama bottoms folded over his stumps. He was quieter. He sat day after day in the summer sun among his roses, staring out at the pebble-dashed walls and the red roofs and the empty sky. The Woodbines dangled in his fingers, "O Sacred Heart" drifted gently from his lips. Mrs. Mickley brought him cups of tea, glasses of beer, Woodbines. Once I stood with Mam at the window and watched Mrs. Mickley stroke her husband's head and gently kiss his cheek.

"She's telling him he's going to get better," said Mam.

We saw the smile growing on Joe Mickley's face.

"That's love," said Mam. "True love."

Slog's dad still joked and called out to anybody passing by.

"Walk?" he'd say. "Man, I cannot even bliddy hop."

"They can hack your body to a hundred bits," he'd say. "But they cannot hack your soul."

We saw him shrinking. Slog told me he'd heard his mother whispering about his dad's fingers coming off. He told me about Mrs. Mickley lifting his dad from the chair each night, laying him down, whispering her good-nights, like he was a little bairn. Slog said that some nights when he was really scared, he got into bed beside them.

"But it just makes it worse," he said. He cried. "I'm bigger than me dad, Davie. I'm bigger than me bliddy dad!"

And he put his arms around me and put his head on my shoulder and cried.

"Slog, man," I said as I tugged away. "Howay, Slogger, man!"

One day late in August, Slog's dad caught me looking. He waved me to him. I went to him slowly. He winked.

"Aye," I muttered.

"Saveloy, I suppose? With everything?"

"Aye. Aye."

I looked out over the pig's head. Slog was with the bloke, looking down at him, talking to him. I saw him lean down to touch the bloke.

"And a dip?" said Billy.

"Aye," I said.

He plunged the sandwich into a trough of gravy.

"Bliddy lovely," he said. "Though I say it myself. A shilling to you, sir."

I paid him but I couldn't go out through the door. The sandwich was hot. The gravy was dripping to my feet.

Billy laughed.

"Penny for them," he said.

I watched Slog get onto the bench beside the bloke.

"Do you believe there's life after death?" I said.

Billy laughed.

"Now there's a question for a butcher!" he said.

A skinny old woman came in past me.

"What can I do you for, pet?" said Billy. "See you, Davie."

He laughed.

23

"Kids!" he said.

Slog looked that happy as I walked toward them. He was leaning on the bloke and the bloke was leaning back on the bench, grinning at the sky. Slog made a fist and a face of joy when he saw me.

"It's Dad, Davie!" he said. "See? I told you."

I stood in front of them.

"You remember Davie, Dad," said Slog.

The bloke looked at me. He looked nothing like the Joe Mickley I used to know. His face was filthy but it was smooth and his eyes were shining bright.

"'Course I do," he said. "Nice to see you, son."

Slog laughed.

"Davie's a bit scared," he said.

"No wonder," said the bloke. "That looks very tasty."

I held the sandwich out to him.

He took it, opened it, and smelt it, looked at the meat and pease pudding and stuffing and mustard and gravy. He closed his eyes and smiled, then lifted it to his mouth.

"Saveloy with everything," he said. He licked the gravy from his lips, wiped his chin with his hand. "Bliddy lovely. You got owt to drink?"

"No," I said.

"Ha. He has got a tongue!"

"He looks a bit different," said Slog. "But that's just cos he's been . . ."

"Transfigured," said the bloke.

"Aye," said Slog. "Transfigured. Can I show him your legs, Dad?"

The bloke laughed gently. He bit his saveloy sandwich. His eyes glittered as he watched me.

"Aye," he said. "Gan on. Show him me legs, son."

And Slog knelt at his feet and rolled the bloke's tattered trouser bottoms up and showed the bloke's dirty socks and dirty shins.

"See?" he whispered.

He touched the bloke's legs with his fingers.

"Aren't they lovely?" he said. "Touch them, Davie."

I didn't move.

"Gan on," said the bloke. "Touch them, Davie."

His voice got colder.

"Do it for Slogger, Davie," he said.

I crouched, I touched, I felt the hair and the skin and the bones and muscles underneath. I recoiled; I stood up again.

"It's true, see?" said Slog. "He got them back in Heaven."

"What d'you think of that, then, Davie?" said the bloke.

Slog smiled.

"He thinks they're bliddy lovely, Dad."

Slog stroked the bloke's legs one more time, then rolled the trousers down again.

"What's Heaven like, Dad?" said Slog.

"Hard to describe, son."

"Please, Dad."

"It's like bright and peaceful, and there's God and the angels and all that. . . ." The bloke looked at his sandwich. "It's like having all the saveloy dips you ever want. With everything, every time."

"It must be great."

"Oh, aye, son. It's dead canny."

"Are you coming to see Mam, Dad?" he said.

The bloke pursed his lips and sucked in air and gazed into the sky.

"Dunno. Dunno if I've got the time, son."

Slog's face fell.

The bloke reached out and stroked Slog's cheek.

"This is very special," he said. "Very rare. They let it happen cos you're a very rare and special lad."

He looked into the sky and talked into the sky.

"How much longer have I got?" he said, then he nodded. "Aye. OK. OK."

He shrugged and looked back at Slog.

"No," he said. "Time's pressing. I cannot do it, son."

There were tears in Slog's eyes.

"She misses you that much, Dad," he said.

"Aye. I know." The bloke looked into the sky again. "How much longer?" he said.

He took Slog in his arms.

"Come here," he whispered.

I watched them hold each other tight.

"You can tell her about me," said the bloke. "You can tell her I love her and miss her and all." He looked at me over Slog's shoulder. "And so can Davie, your best mate. Can't you, Davie? Can't you?"

"Aye," I muttered.

Then the bloke stood up. Slog still clung to him.

"Can I come with you, Dad?" he said.

The bloke smiled.

"You know you can't, son."

"What did you do?" I said.

"Eh?" said the bloke.

"What job did you do?"

The bloke looked at me, dead cold.

"I was a binman, Davie," he said. "I used to stink but I didn't mind. And I followed the stink to get me here."

He cupped Slog's face in his hands.

"Isn't that right, son?"

"Aye," said Slog.

"So what's Slog's mother called?" I said.

"Eh?"

"Your wife. What's her name?"

The bloke looked at me. He looked at Slog. He pushed the last bit of sandwich into his mouth and chewed. A sparrow hopped close to our feet, trying to get at the crumbs. The bloke licked his lips, wiped his chin, stared into the sky.

"Please, Dad," whispered Slog.

The bloke shrugged. He gritted his teeth and sighed and looked at me so cold and at Slog so gentle.

"Slog's mother," he said. "My wife. . . ." He shrugged again. "She's called Mary."

"Oh, Dad!" said Slog, and his face was transfigured by joy. "Oh, Dad!"

The bloke laughed.

"Ha! Bliddy ha!"

He held Slog by the shoulders.

"Now, son," he said. "You got to stand here and watch me go and you mustn't follow."

"I won't, Dad," whispered Slog.

"And you must always remember me."

"I will, Dad."

"And me, you, and your lovely mam'll be together again one day in Heaven."

"I know that, Dad. I love you, Dad."

"And I love you."

And the bloke kissed Slog, and twisted his face at me, then turned away. He started singing "Faith of Our Fathers." He walked across the square, past Myers' pork shop, and turned down onto the High Street. We ran after him then and we looked down the High Street past the people and the cars but there was no sign of him, and there never would be again.

We stood there speechless. Billy Myers came to the doorway of the pork shop with a bucket of bones in his hand and watched us.

"That was me dad," said Slog.

"Aye?" said Billy.

"Aye. He come back, like he said he would, in the spring."

"That's good," said Billy. "Come and have a dip, son. With everything."

We were kids. There were always tales of ghouls and ghosts and monsters going around. In my first school, St. John's, a spooky stone place down by the Tyne, there were fiends waiting in the deep, dark cupboard just past the staffroom door. The ghosts of dead pit men and pit boys, killed in the Felling Pit disaster of 1812, could be seen during winter dusks in the school yard. A madman lived in that abandoned paint works by the river. Some folk had tails hidden beneath their clothes. Strange creatures were said to have been born in the Queen Elizabeth Hospital, creatures that could never be allowed out into the world — half human, half beast, born by weird couplings. When I camped with pals in their gardens — with Tex Flynn or Graham and Charlie Mein — we quaked as we whispered to each other about the witches and demons that waited in the darkness just beyond the thin canvas wall.

Our imaginings were intensified in church, especially during mission week. This happened every year or two, when teams of priests and fierce monks were sent to us. They roamed the streets and glared. They came to our homes to check up on our attendance at Communion or confession. They stood in the pulpit in a crowded St. Patrick's and terrified us with detailed and gory descriptions of hellfire, burning flesh, demons, brimstone, red-hot pokers.

"Beware!" they snarled, gripping the pulpit edge and leaning toward us. "The creatures of Satan truly do walk among us. Perhaps they are with us now! Be alert! Keep away from them! Avoid all sin. Keep your mind on God!"

In this story, May Malone is lapsed — she used to be a Catholic, but she's lost the faith and has left the Church. Just like one of my friends did in real life, when we were eighteen, May stood up in church one day, yelled at the priest that he was a bliddy liar, and stormed out, never to return. To believers, May had put herself into a very perilous position. She was already headed for the fire. Not surprising, then, that there were rumors about her life, her child. . . . about her monster.

May lives in the dark terraced streets at the lower end of Felling, below the railway line. Norman lives in the new flats by Felling Square, Sir Godfrey Thomson Court, where my family lived for several years. I took Norman's surname, Trench (which I like a lot!) from Richard Trench, a nineteenth-century archbishop who wrote a strange and strangely wonderful book called *Notes on the Miracles of Our Lord*. Trench's book is one that I keep around me on the shelves in the shed where I write. Another book that's always nearby is a collection of William Blake's poems. This story was written for a radio series called *Blake's Doors of Perception*. I was invited to take a line or two from Blake and use it as an inspiration, so I chose his poem "The Garden of Love," which contains these lines:

> *And Priests in black gowns were walking their*
> *   rounds,*
> *And binding with briars my joys and desires.*

There are more echoes of Blake in some of the sentences. I like to think that, by the end, Norman's own doors of perception have started to open.

The story was that May Malone had a monster in her house. She kept it in chains. If you went round to the back of the house and put your ear to the wall, you'd hear it groaning. You'd hear it howling at night if you listened hard. There were tales about May and a priest from Blyth. There was a baby, it was said, but the baby was horrible because it was born from such a sin. Even weirder tales were whispered. The Devil himself had come to May and it was the son of Satan living in her house. She'd been with horses, with dogs, with goats. Anyway, whatever it was, you'd risk your body, your sanity, and probably your soul if you got too close.

Norman Trench was ten or eleven at the time. He lived in the new flats in Felling Square. May's house was at the bottom end of Crimea Terrace, not far from the muddy green where the lads played football.

Norman's mam tightened her lips when he asked her about it.

"Them daft tales! Tek nae notice. What's done is done. Just keep away and leave her be."

To look at May you'd never think she had a monster. She was getting on, but she wore tight skirts, she dyed her hair, and she wore high heels that clicked and clacked on the pavements as she hurried along. She was lapsed. Everybody knew the tale of how she'd stood up in church in the middle of Mass and yelled that the priest was a lyin' bliddy bastard, then stormed down the aisle, spat at the altar, and never went again.

You could see people's faces closing down as she dashed through the streets. She hardly spoke to anybody and you could see that nobody wanted to speak to her. Except for some of the blokes, of course, the ones who sighed as she came near, and who couldn't help following with their eyes when she passed by.

Norman was a miserable kind of kid. Aye, he had

some reasons—the brother that'd died at three years old, a dad that'd gone wrong with the drink and ended up in the clink. But everybody's got something to put up with. Norman was just the kind that took it all too seriously.

People used to go, "Cheer up, man! It might never bliddy happen."

And sometimes he'd yell back, "It's happened albliddyready, right! So bugger off!"

Norman thought about illness and death and dying all the time. He thought about the Devil and Hell. And those nightmares! Boiling oil and scorching flames and red-hot pokers and devils' horns. He told the priest about it in confession and the priest sighed. Oh dear. Such fears and dreams were common enough among his flock. We all had such a cross to bear.

The priest leant closer to the grille, trying to get a proper look at Norman.

"Desolation of the heart," he said, "is often a sign of God's call. Do you ever feel you might have a vocation, my son?"

Norman's mam had been through everything that he had been through, of course, and far worse. The difference was, she had a cheerful heart.

"Let's have a smile," she used to say, and Norman would curl his lips up and try to please her, but it just made things worse.

"Oh, son," she'd say. "Don't grow up so sad. God is good, the world is beautiful, and Heaven waits for us."

Made no difference. Norman believed in none of that. He was shutting down, getting ever more miserable. He couldn't stop himself, even when the lads started moaning.

"Why can't you just enjoy yourself, man? You're like a wet bliddy Monday morning."

No wonder they started to turn their backs on him, like he was May Malone, or running away from him and howling, like he was the monster.

It was October when Norman went to May's for the first time. The nights were turning cold and cutting in. He waited till dark, then down he went to the end of Crimea Terrace and into the back lane. He scrambled over the wall into May's backyard. He went to the house wall and pressed his ear to it. Nothing. Maybe a radio somewhere far away. The distant voices of the lads echoing on the green. He concentrated. All he heard was his heart, then the noises of monsters inside himself. He tiptoed to the kitchen window and cupped his hands, peered in and nearly yelled with bliddy fright. But it was just his own staring eyes that goggled back at him. Nothing else.

Next time he went, though, he was sure there was a bit of grunting, a bit of squeaking. May came into the kitchen and made a pot of tea and put some biscuits on a plate. She looked out. Norman pressed right against the back wall. Then she leant up and pulled the curtains shut. Norman climbed back over the wall and stood in the dark at the end of the terrace. He lit the cigarette he'd bought at Wiffen's shop that he'd said was for his mam. A river bell rang. A door clicked open and shut on Crimea Terrace and footsteps hurried up toward town. He drew deeply on the cigarette. He coughed. He stood looking down through the night toward the river. All this is pitching me closer to bliddy Hell, he thought.

"Where you been?" his mam said when he got back in.

"Football," he said. "With the lads."

"Good lad. That might cheer you up, eh? Or mebbe not."

He kept going back to May's. Maybe he had it in his head that he'd be able to go to the lads and say,

"It's true. There is a monster. Come and see," and that that'd sort everything out. But there was nothing, and soon the lads were taking no notice of him at all. It was like they didn't even see him, like he wasn't there. Probably they'd even forgotten all about May's monster.

Then he steps out of Wiffen's one afternoon and there's May Malone right slap bang in front of him. She's wearing a green coat. Her eyes are green, her fingernails bright red.

"So," she says. "What have you got to say for yourself?"

Norman gulps.

"Come along," she says.

"Nothin', Miss Malone."

"Huh! Nothin'. So would you like to see my monster?"

Norman gulps again and blinks.

"Well?"

She doesn't smile. She isn't cross. Her voice is crisp and clear.

"Yes, please, Miss Malone," he says.

"You won't want to be seen walking with me.

Follow me down in five minutes or so. Come to the front door."

And away she clacks.

He smokes his fag as he walks down Crimea Terrace. He's trying to seem nonchalant.

The door's ajar.

"Don't just stand there" comes her voice from inside.

He sidles through and finds her waiting in a narrow corridor. She goggles, gasps, and claps her hands across her mouth.

"Oh no!" she says. "You are in the house of May Malone! Lightning will strike at any moment!"

Then she laughs and tells him to stop his bliddy trembling and come properly in.

Everything is neat and clean, just as she is. Her green coat is hanging from a hook on the wall. There's a door open to a living room. He sees a couple of armchairs, a couple of ashtrays. There's a decanter with what looks like whiskey in it, and two glasses. There's a painting of a Chinese lady on the hall wall. When May closes the front door, the hallway is deeply shadowed, and a red light shines down from upstairs.

She reaches out and takes his hand in hers. He flinches and she holds his hand a little tighter.

"Don't worry," she softly says. "Come with me and see."

She leads him toward a dark door at the back of the house. She hesitates.

"You won't tell a soul, of course," she says. "Will you?"

She squeezes his hand.

"Will you?"

"No, Miss Malone."

"Good, for I am the one who decides who knows."

She turns the handle of the door.

"Now you may meet my boy. His name is Alexander."

It's a small room. Light falls from a skylight in the ceiling. There's a narrow bed against the wall. The boy is sitting on a small blue sofa. His head is slumped onto his shoulder.

May goes to him, kneels beside him, puts her arm around him.

"Alexander," she whispers. "Here is a new visitor for you."

She turns the boy's head to Norman.

He is very pale. One of his eyes is not there at all. The other is very small, and it gleams, as if from a great

42

distance. His mouth is red and crammed with uneven teeth. His legs and arms are shrunken, frail.

"The visitor's name," she whispers, "is . . ."

"Norman," says Norman.

"Norman. Come closer, Norman."

She looks at him.

"Surely you are not going to hesitate now, are you?"

Norman kneels beside them. May lifts one of Alexander's small hands and rests it against Norman's face. Alexander grunts. He squeaks.

"Yes," murmurs May Malone. "Yes, I know, my love."

She smiles.

"Alexander thinks you are very beautiful," she says.

Norman stares into the tiny distant eye. He searches for the boy's distant consciousness.

"And isn't he beautiful, too?" says May. "Isn't he?"

"Yes, Miss Malone," says Norman at last.

"Good. And Alexander says that you are like an angel. Now say hello. Go on. He can hear you, even though it might seem that he can't, just as he can see you."

"Hello," whispers Norman. "Hello, Alexander."

Alexander squeaks.

"See?" says May. "He answers you. He is a boy, just like you. Can you see that?"

"Yes."

"Good. Now sit beside him, Norman. Go on."

Norman does this. Alexander leans against him.

"And he is getting older, just like you," says May. "He needs a friend, just like you. And he needs to play."

She sits on the edge of the bed, facing the two boys. She smooths her skirt over her knees and smiles.

"You're lovely together," she says.

Alexander suddenly turns his face upward. There is a pigeon there, looking down through the skylight. Alexander's mouth purses and he coos.

"Yes!" says May. "A bird! And look at the clouds, Alexander." He slowly, hesitantly, raises his hands and he opens them over his head. They flutter and tremble in the air.

"See?" says May Malone. "He knows that the world is beautiful, Norman."

Alexander trembles, and Norman can feel the excitement rushing through the boy as the bird flutters its wings above.

"Now," says May. "I would like you to take him out, Norman."

Norman catches his breath. He glances at the door and gets ready to run.

"Please do not leave us," says May Malone. "Not now."

She takes his hand again.

"Just take him out into the yard at first," she says. "What could be so difficult about that?"

"Who's his father?" Norman dares to say.

"You are a nosey bugger, aren't you?"

"Sorry, Miss Malone."

"Are you a churchgoer?"

"Yes."

"I thought so. Those black-gowned bloody priests. They blasted me. Don't let them blast you, Norman, with their *Thou shalt nots*." She touches her boy's head. "They said this angel is a devil. Never mind his father. Will you take him out?"

They help Alexander to rise from the sofa. May Malone opens the door. Norman holds Alexander's arm and guides him out into the place where he's only ever hidden in the dark. It is late afternoon. The sun is descending in the west. There are great streaks of red and gold across the sky. A storm of starlings sweeps over them from north to south. The city rumbles, the river bell rings, the lads' voices echo from the green. Norman imagines walking toward them with May Malone's monster at his side. He imagines the lads turning to him in amazement. He imagines May Malone watching them all from a bench nearby. Alexander reaches upward, upward and he moans with joy. He leans against Norman and coos into his ear. May Malone watches from the doorway.

"See? It's easy enough, isn't it?" she says.

They soon go back inside. They take Alexander to his room and lay him down on the bed.

"He's tired out," said May. "But can you see how he is smiling, Norman?"

"Yes," says Norman, for he can. The distant gleam of Alexander's eye has grown brighter.

"He is as he is because he is as he is," says May. "No other reason. And he is quite as capable of joy as any of us. More so, in fact."

She leans toward Norman.

"You, for instance," she says, "must stop being so sad. You know that, don't you?"

"Yes, Miss Malone."

"Just open your eyes, Norman. The world is a strange and gorgeous and astonishing place."

She looks at her watch.

"Now," she says. "You will come back again, won't you?"

"Yes, Miss Malone."

"And you won't tell anybody, will you? Not until we're ready."

"No, Miss Malone."

"Good."

She kisses his cheek. He says good-bye to Alexander, and she leads him to the door.

"Good night," she says. "Until the next time. We will be waiting for you."

Norman walks up Crimea Terrace below the astonishing sky. He keeps touching his cheek where May Malone's lipstick is, where the memory of her lips is. He remembers the feeling of her red-fingernailed hand upon his. He keeps remembering Alexander's trembles of excitement.

A man is hurrying down the street, with the rim of his trilby tilted over his eyes.

"Hello," says Norman.

The man flinches, looks at the boy in astonishment, then he gives a broad grin.

"Aye, aye, lad," he says, and he winks.

Norman keeps going. All the sadness is lifting away from him as he goes uphill, like he's opening up; like he's beginning to see this world for the first time.

This story is filled with real people: my sisters Mary and Margaret; their friend Cathleen; Cathleen's mother; my mother; my mate Tex Flynn; the footballers Dave Hilley and Alan Suddick. And I suppose, as the narrator is called Davie, I'm in it too. Of course, as soon as you start to write about somebody, you start to fictionalize them. The person in real life isn't quite the same as the person in the tale. And the events in the tale, of course, never happened at all.

It's set on a small estate where we moved when I was eleven, by which time I'd passed my 11-plus and was at grammar school in Hebburn. Until then we'd lived on the council estate beside the new bypass, and then in a new council flat close to Felling Square. Now we were in the first and only house my parents ever bought. It was a short walk uphill from the square, in a ring of semi-detached houses formed by two streets, Coldwell Park Avenue and Coldwell Park Drive. The neighborhood in the story isn't exactly like those streets. There was no gate in Cathleen's garden that led to the park and the playing fields, but there needed to be one for the story, so I put it there. That's a strange thing about writing stories — you put in something imaginary to make the whole thing seem more real.

I always loved football. For a time, I took a football everywhere I went. I dribbled it along the pavements, played keep-up in the back garden, kicked it about with my friends in the streets, on the patches of grass near our homes, in the fields around the town. Sometimes there'd just be a couple of us playing against a garage door, or a handful of us playing in somebody's little garden. Other times, teams of twenty or more would charge across the fields above the town. At the best of times we'd play all day, until we could no longer see the ball, then I'd walk home through the gathering dusk and sleep, and dream I was playing again.

I was crazy about Newcastle United. I roared them on at St. James's Park. I collected photos, posters, programs. I had a black-and-white scarf and a black-and-white hat. I used to go with my mates, Tex Flynn or Peter Varley, maybe, to watch the team training on Hunter's Moor at Spital Tongues. Sometimes we jogged alongside them in the streets around St. James. I remember one day trotting past the shops in Fenham for a few hundred yards with Colin "Cannonball" Taylor, a stocky left winger with the hardest shot I'd ever seen. He teased me, letting me think I could keep pace with him, then laughed fondly and pelted away. I kept scrapbooks with signed photographs and match reports in them. It was such a thrill to stand beside the players, show them my books, watch them sign their names. I used to dream of playing with them: taking a pass from Dave Hilley on my thigh before lashing it into the net, sending an inch-perfect cross onto Alan Suddick's head.

I'd been brought up to believe that God was everywhere, and was always watching us. Maybe it's inevitable that I'd come to write a tale like this, one that turns my boyhood heroes into saints, and in which God seems to wander into an ordinary Felling garden.

The story has gone through a number of incarnations and has been rewritten several times. This latest version, set in a time of snow and ice, seems to work best of all. But maybe it'll seek another rewrite. Some stories seem never to be finished; seem always to be on the point of change.

When God came to Cathleen's garden

A Tuesday morning at the start of the Christmas holidays. Deep fresh snow lay on the ground and the sun was blazing down but I was pretty fed up. I'd packed a flask of tea and some sandwiches and crisps. I had my photograph albums and autograph albums and pens. I was supposed to be going to Newcastle with Tex Flynn. The plan was we'd watch the United players training and get some autographs. In those days you could wander about on the training ground with them. You could jog with them through the streets. They were brilliant and famous, they played

in front of thirty thousand fans every week, but there they were right beside us. They played keep-up, head tennis, penalties, shots. They were always laughing and playing daft tricks on each other, but suddenly one of them would do something that seemed impossible. Sometimes they'd let us join in. They'd fall down when we dribbled past them, they'd dive the wrong way when we took penalties. They'd pretend to be amazed by our tricks, to be terrified by the power of our shots. They didn't keep the magic to themselves. One day Alan Suddick showed me how to swerve the ball with the outside of my foot. Dave Hilley told me it wasn't power that made a great shot, it was timing. He spent more than ten minutes with me, passing the ball to me, telling me to fire it back. "That's good, son," he said. "You'll get there. Practice, practice, practice, till you can do it without a thought." Lots of lads went, especially in the holidays. We all had autograph books and albums packed with photos we'd cut out of the papers. The players were great. They all signed our books. *Best wishes,* they wrote, or *Keep on kicking* or *Have a great life!*

But Tex had gone down with flu, which seemed pretty weird. He'd been fine on Monday afternoon.

"Are you sure?" I asked his mam when she answered the door with the news.

"Sure?" she said. "You want to go and see him and catch it yourself?"

I looked past her into the shadowy hall. I thought of his bedroom above. It was just like mine: black-and-white stripes everywhere, stacks of old football programs, photographs of the heroes pinned to the walls. I thought of him lying there, sweating and shivering and taking Beecham's Powders and drinking orange juice and sniffing Vicks.

"But he was fine," I said.

"Aye, he was, Davie. Till he got to playing football in a blooming blizzard. Till he got back here in the pitch-black freezing cold, soaking wet and shuddering. A fine Christmas he's going to have, isn't he?"

"Yes, Mrs. Flynn."

"Yes, Mrs. Flynn! Huh! Anyway, they'll not be training today, not if they've got any sense."

And she said good-bye and shut the door.

I walked back home up Felling Bank. Not be training? Of course they would, just like me. I kicked a stone through the slush on the pavement. I dribbled it around the lampposts and telegraph poles. I heard the crowd all around me, yelling me on. I heard them singing "The Blaydon Races." In my head I said, "He's beaten one man! He's beaten two! Can he do it?" I sidestepped a little dog that came out of nowhere. I dropped my shoulder, slid on a patch of ice, swerved one way, then another, and flicked the stone through an open gate. I slithered to a stop and punched the air. I raised my arms to the sky. "Yes! Yeeeees! What a goal!" And the dog danced and yapped around me.

Back at home, in the garden, I kicked the snow aside, sat on the back step and swigged some of the tea. I told my mam about Tex.

"That's the flu for you," she said. "One minute you're as right as rain, the next you're a shivering wreck."

"He was fine yesterday," I said.

"Yes, but I don't expect that playing football in a—"

"It was just a bit of snow!"

"And how would you like it, just before Christmas? The poor lad."

She folded her arms and looked down at me.

"Now I hope you're not going to be moping all day."

I tugged my black-and-white scarf around my neck. I pulled down my black-and-white hat. I got one of

my albums out. I'd just stuck some new pictures in.
There was a brilliant one from the *Pink:* Dave lashing
in the winner against Swansea City under the headline
HILLEY SINKS THE SWANS. There was an even better
one of Alan. He was horizontal, four feet off the
ground. His eyes were bright with concentration. The
ball had just left his head and was on its way to the goal.
His arms were spread wide, just like he was flying.
Alan Suddick. Dave Hilley. They could do anything.

I played with my new biro and dreamt I was a
famous player. I imagined kids lining up in front of
me. I scribbled my name fast on scraps of paper.

"That's OK, son," I murmured. "It's a pleasure, lad."

I drank my tea, chewed my sandwiches, crunched
the crisps. My breath drifted in the icy air. Maybe Tex
was just putting it on, I thought. Maybe he was going
off the team. Maybe he was going off me.

Lads' voices echoed across the roofs from the playing
fields outside the estate.

"On me head! On me head!"

"Get stuck in!"

"Goal! Goal! Yeeeeees!"

I kept listening. Somebody was playing a trumpet
somewhere. Somebody was banging a drum.

Mam came out again.

"You're wasting a beautiful winter's day," she said. "There's a million things you could do instead of sitting there and staring into space."

"A million?" I said.

"Yes."

"Like what?"

"You could go and play football with the lads. You could shovel some of that snow off the front path."

"That's two," I said.

"You watch your lip," she said. "One thing you could certainly do is stop staring at those daft pictures. There's nothing special about those fellers. They're people, just like you."

She went back in. What did she mean, just like me? She hadn't seen Dave Hilley dribble. She hadn't seen an Alan Suddick free kick. These "fellers" could work miracles! I closed my eyes. I tried to feel like Alan when he smashed the ball into the net. I tried to feel like Dave when he left a defender sprawling in the dirt. I practised Dave's signature until it was just like his. I wrote, *To Davie. Best wishes, Dave Hilley* on his picture.

"Thanks, Dave," I said.

I said, "You're welcome, son," in Dave's gentle Scottish accent.

I signed Alan's picture, *To Davie, a true fan. Yours in sport. Alan Suddick.*

I winked like Alan did.

"No bother, lad," I whispered.

I sat there, in the icy sunshine, in the dream.

Then there were footsteps and two of my sisters—Mary and Margaret—were there, wrapped up in their brown winter coats with wellies on their feet.

"What do you want?" I grunted.

Mary put her finger to her lips.

"Shh," she said.

Mam waved at them through the kitchen window. They waved back.

"It's a *secret,*" Margaret whispered.

I sighed.

"What is?"

They turned so that Mam couldn't see their faces.

"God's come," said Mary.

"What?" I said.

"God's come. He's in Cathleen Kelly's garden," said Mary. "He was fast asleep and now he's woke up and he's sitting by the fish pond. Are you coming to see?

Cathleen said you should, but nobody else."

I rolled my eyes. What a pair.

"Please," said Margaret. "And hurry up, before he goes away."

I sighed again. Mam would have me shoveling that snow if I didn't do something soon. So I stood up. I still had my album and my biro in my hand. Mam waved as we left.

We headed down toward Cathleen's. I flung a couple of snowballs at some kids I knew across the street.

"How do you know it's God?" I said.

"Cathleen says it must be," said Mary. "She's been saying loads of prayers since Jasper died. She's been begging him to help her. And he's sitting just where Jasper's buried."

"And he looks *just* like his pictures," said Margaret.

"And he appeared like magic," said Mary. "Out of nothing."

"So it's true," said Margaret. "Isn't it?"

I flung some more snowballs. How did I know?

We went into Cathleen's front gate and down the side of her house and into the back garden. Cathleen was kneeling on a shopping bag in the snow beside the little fish pond with her hands joined. Mary and

Margaret pulled their coats over their knees, knelt down beside her and joined their hands too, as if they were in church. Mary looked at me like she thought I should kneel as well, but I didn't.

God was sitting on a folded blanket in the sunshine with his legs crossed. You could see how he'd shoved away the snow with his boots.

"This is Davie, Lord," said Cathleen.

God looked at me and smiled.

He had dark skin and dark eyes. He wore thick orange robes and brown leather boots. He had a black cap on but you could see he was bald. He had a pot-belly and a big white beard.

He raised a hand in greeting. I nodded at him.

"Do your mam and dad know?" I asked Cathleen.

She shook her head.

"Dad's at work," she said. "Mam's doing some Christmas shopping."

"Does he talk?" I said.

"We don't know."

God smiled. He picked a stone up from the edge of the pond. He showed it in his hand, closed his hand, then opened it again, and the stone had gone. Then he took the same stone out of his left ear and put it back by the pond again. Margaret clapped. God reached into the snow, found a stick, snapped it, and put it back together again. He took another stick as long as his arm and opened his mouth and swallowed it and drew it out again.

He smiled and giggled, and the girls clapped.

I saw tears in Cathleen's eyes.

She clasped her hands tight and leant right toward God.

"Please, Lord," she said.

He turned his face toward her. She chewed her lips.

"I see your powers, Lord," she whispered. "Please, Lord, could you possibly bring Jasper back to us?"

God smiled. He reached up, plucked something from the empty air, then showed a handful of tiny silver coins to us. He dropped them into Margaret's hands.

"Please," Cathleen begged. "Please. I know you can."

He formed a little creature from a handful of snow, tossed it up into the air, and off it flew, a silver bird. He smiled at Cathleen. He stretched and yawned. He rested his hands on his potbelly and turned his face toward the sun.

Everything was still. There were streaks of pink in the blue sky. The air shimmered, the snow and ice glowed. I heard the trumpet again, high-pitched and far away. God heard it too. He tilted his head, listened and smiled. There was a gate at the back of Cathleen's garden that led to a park and then to the playing fields. Kids were yelling out there. There were mad cries from the lads as a goal was scored.

"Yes! It's in! Yeeeees!"

I looked at God and knew he wasn't God. His clothes were faded and patched. His boots were held together with string. His face was filthy. He looked like he'd walked miles. He was just some weird bloke that'd wandered in from the park for a nap in the shade.

I felt so stupid. I should have gone and played football. I should have gone to Newcastle on my own.

"We should tell somebody about him," I said.

"But who?" said Mary.

"Father O'Mahoney?" said Margaret. "Or the Pope, maybe?"

"No!" said Cathleen. "He came to *my* garden. He came just for us. Can you, Lord? Please, Lord. Please bring Jasper back."

I was stuck. I couldn't just clear off and leave them here with him.

"When's your mam coming back?" I said to Cathleen.

She just kept on staring at God.

God brushed the snow away from the ice at the edges of the pond. We saw goldfish shining in the depths. He broke the ice and dipped his hand in and let water trickle from his hand across his brow. Then he held his hand toward us. Cathleen reached out. She caught some drops and touched them to her own brow. God smiled at her. He opened his mouth, took three goldfish out of it, showed them to us, and slid them gently down into the water, where they flickered and flashed.

"Will you sign my book?" I said.

God raised his eyebrows.

"They're all footballers in here," I said. "They play for Newcastle. But there's an empty page you could use."

I knelt down beside him. He smelt spicy and sweet, like the stuff Mam puts into the Christmas pudding.

I opened the book and God's eyes widened.

"They're footballers," I said.

God laughed softly and pointed to Alan.

"That's Alan Suddick, God," I said. "He's brilliant! And so's Dave Hilley. Look, that's him scoring the winner against Swansea."

God ran his fingers over Alan's face, over Dave's face. He smiled, as if he knew them well.

I showed him where it said *To Davie. Best wishes, Dave Hilley.*

"That's how the footballers do it," I said. "Will you write that? And will you sign it from God?"

I handed him the new biro. He smiled as he clicked the point in and out and in and out. He held it to his ear to listen to the clicks. He ran his fingers across the page in the book as if he loved the feel of it. He listened to the distant trumpet for a moment. Then he licked his lips and started to copy: *To Davie. Best wishes.* He concentrated hard, but he couldn't hold the pen properly, and his writing was all uneven and clumsy. He looked at what he'd written. It looked like:

7o Douic Bes4 N|L5Htes

He shrugged, as if to say he was sorry but it was the best he could do.

"That's great, Lord," I said. "Thank you. Will you put your name now, please?"

He put the pen on the page again. I held his cold, smooth hand this time. I guided him as he wrote, *God.*

I read the words out loud. God giggled. I giggled with him.

"Now you're there in the book with Alan and Dave," I said.

Cathleen was furious. She glared at Mary and Margaret.

"I hope you two aren't going to ask for something now!" she whispered. "This is *my* garden!"

Mary and Margaret shook their heads.

"Good," said Cathleen. "Please, God. *Please!*"

I sighed. She might as well ask Alan or Dave to bring her dog back. I looked at a photo of Alan leaping over a clumsy defender. I looked at Dave balancing the ball on his knee. I closed my eyes and imagined kneeling before them on the training ground. *Please, Alan. Please, Dave. Please bring Jasper back again.*

I thought of Jasper. He was an ordinary little black-and-white dog. A jumpy, yappy, happy thing, part spaniel, part poodle, part something else. He'd come from a big litter from somewhere on Brettanby Road. He was just a few years old, but some disease got into him and there was no saving him. Mr. Watkinson, the vet in Felling Square, had put him down. I'd seen Cathleen and her mam bringing him back in a brown shopping bag. Mary and Margaret had seen Cathleen's dad digging his grave. Sometimes at night I thought of him lying there, his little body turning, like all bodies, to dust, to earth.

God smiled at Cathleen. There was great kindness in his eyes. He stood up and rubbed his knees and his back as if they were aching. He picked up his blanket and put it over his shoulder. He stretched and yawned. He stroked his beard, like he was wondering about something, then put his hand deep into his robes and took out a little box. There was a picture of a beautiful faraway mountainous place on it. He opened it, and there were sweets inside. He held them out to us. They were delicious, soft and mysteriously sweet, and dusted with the finest sugar.

We licked our lips at their deliciousness.

"They're lovely, God!" said Mary.

He put the whole box into her hands. Then he raised his hand as if in farewell.

"But where are you going?" asked Cathleen.

"Aaaaah," said God.

It was the first thing we'd heard him say.

"And what about Jasper?" said Cathleen.

"Aaaaah," he said again, but much more sadly.

She jabbed her finger toward the earth.

"He's down there in the hard cold ground!" she said.

"And I've been praying to you and praying to you and praying to you!"

God looked down at the earth beside the pond. He spread his hands and closed his eyes. He squeezed Cathleen gently on the shoulder, then he just turned and walked through the gate into the park.

He walked slowly and easily, rocking gently from side to side. He walked across the playing fields. Children ran to him across the ice and snow. He kept reaching into his robes, taking things out, giving them to the children.

Cathleen stamped her foot.

"See? Every single person gets something!" she said. "You get silver coins, you get sweets, you get his autograph, they get what he's giving them. And what do I get? Absolutely nothing!"

She yelled after God.

"What about Jasper? What about my *dog*?"

God didn't turn.

"You don't care!" she yelled. "I don't believe in you!"

He hesitated, but he didn't turn.

Cathleen stamped again, then realized she was stamping right on top of Jasper. It just made her cry some more.

"Oh!" she yelled. "Why don't all you silly people just go home?"

But we didn't. We shared the sweets. I wished I had a picture of God to go with his autograph.

Someone thumped the far-off drum.

After a while I said, "It wasn't really God, you know."

Cathleen stamped her feet again. She raised her fists in the air.

"I know that!" she said. "Do you think I don't know that?"

I kept thinking I should go, but I didn't. I bet Tex has had a miraculous recovery, I thought. I bet he's out playing football right now.

"Was it not God, Mary?" whispered Margaret.

Mary shook her head.

"No. Of course not. Shh."

The sun fell lower and the sky above Felling began to glow red and gold.

Soon, Cathleen's mam came home, loaded down with shopping bags.

"Hello, everybody," she said. "And Davie as well! Hello, stranger."

She handed custard creams around and took a leaflet from her handbag.

"Town's full of funny folk giving these out," she said. "Look what's on its way."

A circus. There were pictures of a big top, a pony, a tiger, a girl swinging on a trapeze.

And on the back there it was, a picture of God in his orange robes and boots and with his great white beard.

THE MISTERIOUS SWAMI,
THE GREAT ORIENTIAL MAGICIAN
SEE SWAMI, AND YOU WILL BELEIVE IN MIRACLES!

Margaret gasped. Cathleen put her tongue out at me. She flicked some crumbs from her lips. I was already imagining the picture stuck in my book close to the pictures of Dave and Alan. Maybe I could find Swami again and get him to sign it with his real name.

"Is everything all right, love?" said Mrs. Kelly to Cathleen.

"Yes!" snapped Cathleen.

Mrs. Kelly smiled. She put her arm around Cathleen. The trumpet and drum echoed through the late afternoon air.

"Oh, love," she said softly. "Jasper loved you very much, you know."

Mrs. Kelly looked me in the eye and I knew she wanted us to leave.

"Come on," I said to my sisters, and we all got up.

We were heading down by the side of the house when the barking started.

"What's that?" said Mary.

"It's Jasper!" gasped Margaret.

"Don't be silly," I said.

But we all looked back. The barking came from the other side of the gate into the park. We could hear paws scratching and scratching there. We could hear the dog flinging itself against the gate. We stepped back into the garden.

"Somebody sounds very excited," said Mrs. Kelly.

The dog barked and yapped and yelped.

"Go away!" she said, but it barked and barked.

"Do we dare to let it in?" she said.

Margaret clasped her hands together. She closed her eyes tight and tilted her face toward the sky.

"I'll go," said Cathleen at last. "I'm the one that's good with dogs, aren't I?"

She wiped the tears from her eyes with her sleeve. She went to the gate. She stood on tiptoes and looked over it.

"Oh!" she cried.

She looked back at us with amazement in her eyes. Then turned to the dog again.

"Oh, welcome home!" she cried.

And she opened the gate and the little yappy black-and-white dog raced in.

I didn't think this would turn out to be a ghost story. I knew it'd be a tale about an outsider, a boy separated from other kids by his appearance, by his background, by what others took to be his stupidity. I knew he'd be nicknamed "The Missing Link" and he'd go through a lot of trouble. Once the story got going, it developed its own momentum and the ending seemed inevitable.

Back then, everyone took the 11-plus exam. If you passed, you went to grammar school. If you didn't, you were classed as a failure and you went to secondary modern. I had lots of friends and relatives who didn't pass — good, decent, bright boys and girls who at the age of eleven were already classed as failures, whose whole lives would be affected by this. And for some of them it was family circumstances, deprivation, poverty, or illness that robbed them of this chance.

I passed and went to a Catholic grammar school in Hebburn, three miles downriver from Felling.

The boys in the story know they're supposed to feel clever, but they often don't. They try to adopt a pose of superiority, but it isn't tempered by compassion. Their toughness is a sham. As the narrator says, bullying was commonplace back then. Kids who were bullied were expected to toughen up, to laugh it off, or to just put up with it. The ones who showed signs of weakness were bullied even more.

There was always a tension between education and religion. The more you learned and the more you read and the more you matured, the more you started to question and to doubt. You began to doubt both the scary things (dominated by Satan, his devils, and Hell) and the comforting things (dominated by Jesus, his angels, and Heaven). This was scary indeed, because you were told that doubt was a dangerous thing. It might lead you from the one true path. It was scary even to *admit* to doubt. It was strange. We were learning about the universe, evolution, the human mind. How did such things tie in with what we were told in church or in our RE lessons? What did the Hail Mary mean to us, modern adolescents in a modern world?

But the faith still held us. We went to Mass and Communion and confession. We went along to services (like the novena services in the story) that promised to save our souls. Yes, we were tempted to say it was all a lot of nonsense, but we didn't dare. As the boys in the story know, and as the Hail Mary emphasizes, the hour of death is mightily important. *Holy Mary, Mother of God, pray for us sinners, now and at the hour of our death . . .* Will you be in a state of grace? Will you be prepared for Final Judgment? Will a priest be nearby to hear your last confession? Our childhoods and adolescence were laced with such questions.

In that world, bullying and tormenting a boy like Christopher McNally was a far lesser sin than, say, missing Sunday Mass or taking God's name in vain. Our duties to retain the faith and to please and obey God were much more important than our duty to love and to care for our fellow creatures.

I wrote this story for an evening of ghost story readings at the Lit & Phil in Newcastle. (Its full name is the Literary and Philosophical Society

of Newcastle upon Tyne.) This is a wonderful
Georgian library near the middle of town, with high,
bright book-filled rooms on the ground floor and
appropriately spooky rooms below. It is democratic
and open to everyone, founded on the belief that
every single one of us is a worthwhile citizen, that
each of us can read, learn, flourish, and play
an active part in our amazing world.
It's where I often go to write. It's
where I've just written this.

the missing link

It started when they came to town. There were just two of them, McNally and his mother. They seemed to come from nowhere, but it turned out they harked from West Ham, West Bromwich, somewhere like that. The story was, there'd been some trouble—nobody was sure what—and they were looking for a fresh start.

They came to Jonadab. It was a half-abandoned place down by the Tyne: all knocked-down streets and shuttered shops and boarded houses. It was the time of the slum clearances, families getting shifted from the old Victorian terraces and into the new pebble-dashed estates farther up the hill. Jonadab was almost gone. There were just a few families waiting to get re-housed. The McNallys would have to wait their turn. They'd be the last in line.

The mother was a little hunch-shouldered, weary-looking woman with the scar of some old wound on her face. She got work at Swan Hunter's shipyard: a cleaner, the lowest of the low, sweeping out the ships after the caulkers and welders and burners, mopping out the bogs.

There must've been a dad at one time, but there was no sign of him.

"He must have upped and offed," said my mate Nixon. "Or slit his wrists more likely. And who could bliddy blame him? A woman like that. A son like that. Bliddy Hell. Just imagine it."

We couldn't believe it when the lad arrived at school. The school was St. Aidan's, a grammar school. We'd all passed the 11-plus. We were the bright ones, we were the chosen few. And now here came this ugly, stupid-looking thing. He was big and lumpy. Bulbous eyes. There was always dribble on his chin. He'd got a uniform from somewhere: crumpled trousers, worn-down shoes, a tight and tatty, worn-out blazer with the school badge peeling from the pocket. He stank, of course. And that voice! It was so weird and ugly he hardly dared to use it: stupid-sounding, thick and wet, half a grunt and half a whine, whistly and wobbly.

"Jesus bliddy Christ," said Nixon in disgust. "How the hell did a thing like that get let into a place like this?"

We'd started doing science, of course. We'd already found out about evolution. We loved the idea that we were all descended from apes, that everything had led to us, to clever *Homo sapiens;* that we were striding forward together into a bright new world. And now here was Christopher McNally. We took one look at him and pretty soon we were hooting and grunting. We were dangling our fists down to the ground and pretending to be throwbacks or thick.

I was the one who came up with his name. It was during English. We were writing about Shakespeare or somebody like that. I looked across and saw McNally dribbling, saw the way he clutched the pen with his clumsy fingers, the way his head rocked as he wrote. He was hardly human. I gagged, and nearly retched.

I nudged Nixon.

"It's him," I whispered.

"Who?" said McNally.

I stifled my sniggers. I nodded toward McNally.

"The Missing Link," I said. "We've found the Missing Link at last."

From then on, we were poking him with sticks, chucking bananas at him. The size of him, he could've taken any of us, but he never lifted a finger, and never said a word.

"It's like he thinks he deserves it," Nixon said.

"He does!" we said, and we mocked some more.

There was a little bit of pity from the girls. Some of them said we should be ashamed of ourselves. They even said it was us that was half evolved. But it didn't last long. It was hard for them to keep on feeling sorry for hunched shoulders and hairy moles and a grunty voice and smelly breath.

And the teachers? Well, they were different days. Bullying was everywhere. There was neither blood nor broken bones, so they managed to turn their eyes away, and to see next to nowt.

Soon after McNally arrives, we're in the school hall with the priest. You wouldn't believe it nowadays but back then it was all that ancient stuff about fighting temptation and avoiding sin, and about how God sees everything, even our most secret thoughts. It was all to make sure we kept our hands off the girls, of course. Not that it worked very well. Every year there were fifth-formers and sixth-formers slinking off with bairns in their bellies. Anyway, the lads are rolling their eyes like always, and the girls are blushing and sniggering and staring at their nails. Then we get the catechism for the millionth time: *Who made you?* Blah blah blah. Blah blah blah. *Why did God make you?* Blah blah blah. Then the dire warnings:

What if death came now, this very second?

Are you in a state of grace?

Are you prepared for Final Judgment?

The Final Judgment. My God, we still believed in that. Or even if we said we didn't, we were still half terrified of it.

"Hell lies in wait," they said. "How will you keep yourself away from it?"

Anyway, Link's at the back. We can hear his grunty breath, and it's like there's some weird snuffling beast among us.

Nixon pipes up.

"Have all creatures got souls, Father?"

"All creatures?" says the priest.

"Yes, Father. Even them from way, way back, like the apes and the half-human things we grew from and that?"

We all start nudging, giggling. We all start turning and looking at Link.

The priest sighs.

"An interesting question. But you are leaping into dark theological waters, my son. What is certain is that we have souls, and we must fortify them. Which leads me to my main topic — to introduce you to the First Friday Novena."

Novenas. We were always doing sodding novenas. Don't know what it was about the number nine, but we were always saying nine prayers for this and nine for that. We'd light nine candles in a row. We'd contemplate the nine orders of angels and the nine rivers of Hell. And this one?

"This novena," says the priest, "may be the most powerful of all. You must come to Mass and take Holy Communion on the first Friday of the month, for nine months in a row."

He pauses. We wait for whatever reward will be promised.

"Do this," he says, "and the hour of your death will not arrive without a priest being close at hand to administer the blessed sacrament."

We all listen. We know what that could mean. No matter what sins we have committed, a priest will be there to take our last confession, to give us his blessing. We will be kept out of the jaws of Hell.

"None of us is perfect," he whispers. "But do we not all dream of dying without a trace of sin on our souls? This novena helps that dream come true."

"Is it true?" asks someone.

"There is no infallible teaching. But the devout have always observed this novena, and many of our greatest saints. Isn't it better to be safe than sorry?" He peers at us. "Or perhaps you would prefer to take a risk. Perhaps you would prefer to toy with the fires of destruction."

Before he leaves, he says, "I see we have a new boy. What's your name, lad?"

Link grunts something. We all squeeze our eyes and hold our laughter in.

"He's the Missing Link," squeaks Nixon.

Our laughter bursts free.

The priest shakes his head.

"Take no notice, my son," he says. He pats Link

on the arm as he leaves. "You'll find they're not all badness. You'll surely find a pal among them."

He rolls his eyes.

"You lot! What are we going to do with you?" he says. "We begin this Friday. Don't forget."

We didn't forget. The church was full, and there we were, breakfasts in brown paper bags, stomachs groaning, souls yearning, tongues stuck out to welcome Christ's body and salvation into ourselves.

And there was Link, kneeling just along the altar rail from us.

"Who does he bliddy think he is?" muttered Nixon at my side. He groaned in disgust as the priest pressed the pure white host onto Link's horrible lumpy tongue.

"Novena?" he said. "I'll bliddy novena him."

After Mass, we waited in an alleyway between the church and the school. We dragged Link in and started on him.

That morning saw the first of the monthly beatings of the missing link between the age of stupid apes and the age of brainy men.

★   ★   ★

I don't know why he came to me. I was always there, those Friday mornings in the alleyway. I wasn't the worst of us, but I always did my bit. And I always urged the others on. I always laughed at Nixon — the way he slapped and poked and kicked and spat, leaving pain and fright but neither blood nor broken bones. I was always there hooting with laughter as Link scuttled off.

But it was me that Link came to, in the school yard, one bright and early morning. There was hardly anybody else around. I must've still been half asleep. I felt the touch on my shoulder. I turned round and Link was there, his wet eyes looking down at me, his tongue flapping in his horrible wet mouth.

I couldn't catch his words at first.

"Eh?" I said.

"It's an illness," he grunted.

I looked around, backed away.

"Eh?" I said.

"The thing that makes me h-horrible," he said. "Look at how me arms and legs is thickening and me chin's dropping."

He showed his thick, muscly, lumpy limbs, his grotesque chin, the hairs sprouting on his face.

"And me tongue," he said. "It's too big for me mouth. It's why I . . ."

"What're the doctors doing?" I said.

He took a big purple pill out. He shoved it in his mouth and swallowed it.

"The novena'll help and all," he said. "I'm praying for deliverance from it."

He swiped his sleeve across his mouth.

"D'you believe me?" he said.

"Dunno," I said.

Link moved closer. He reached out to me, held me by the collar, breathed on me with his rotten breath.

"Look through this," he said. "Look through all the ugliness."

I tried to pull away.

Beyond him, I saw Nixon swaggering through the school gates.

"Look right inside," said Link. "I'm just like you."

"Like what?" I said.

"Aye, like y-you."

Nixon quickened toward us. He started grinning.

"Hey, Nixon," I said. "I'm just having a nice chat with the Missing Link."

"Ah, isn't that nice," said Nixon.

"I know," I said. "And listen—Link says he's just like us."

"Is that right?" said Nixon.

"Aye," I said.

"Then Link," said Nixon, "is even stupider than we thought."

Link took his hand away from me. We laughed and watched him shuffle off.

We went round the back and lit a fag.

"What's he doing coming to you?" said Nixon.

"Mebbe he thinks I'll be his pal."

Nixon laughed.

"Funny, eh? You always look as sweet as pie. Mothers and old biddies and missing links think you're the bee's bliddy knees. They don't see to the inside. Not like I do."

I drew on the fag and showed my teeth.

"They don't," I said. "I'm a bliddy devil, eh?"

Even so, I think I did start to change that day. I thought about being dragged out of West Bromwich to a place like this; having no father, having a mother like that, having some horrible condition; being scared of what's happening to your own body; being all alone at school;

being scared of kids that should be your mates.

But what good's change if it's all inside yourself and nowt happens on the outside? What's the good of knowing that you shouldn't do something like beating up Link when you go on doing it? What's the use of it when your mate Nixon comes and tells you you're going to stop the Missing Link from finishing his novena, and you just answer, "Aye! That's a great idea! That'll be a real bliddy laugh!"

The trouble is, it's easy to go along with it all. And it's a laugh, especially when you get to plotting with your mates.

"Novena?" you say. "Ha! We'll bliddy novena him!"

Early morning, first Friday, ninth month. It was November, still dark, icy cold. We waited, half a dozen of us, in a deep doorway on the High Street. We smoked Woodbines and thought about salvation, and resisted the temptation to eat our breakfasts there and then. We felt good. We were going to escape the jaws of Hell today.

"Link alert!" whispered somebody at last, and there he was, lurching up from Jonadab beneath the streetlights.

We did it fast. He hardly struggled. We dragged him down the alleyway into a little abandoned printing shop. We tied him to a twisted doorframe and gagged him with his scarf. He kept his eyes on me but I did nothing while Nixon softly whispered, "Don't worry, Link. We'll soon be back to let you go."

We hurried churchward under heavy, sleety-looking clouds. Inside, we hung our heads and murmured the prayers. At the altar rail I cast my eyes over the ornate altar, the saints in their little niches, the crucifix, the monstrance. I felt no connection to any of it. I told myself I believed none of it. I stared through to the emptiness behind it all, then opened my mouth and stuck out my tongue when the priest came to me. I closed my eyes, felt the bread pressed onto my tongue then swallowed it down into the emptiness inside myself.

Afterward, we clenched our fists in triumph at achieving our novenas.

"Hell is defeated!" said Nixon.

Then we went back to the alleyway to liberate the Missing Link.

He died in mid-December. We were hanging baubles on the classroom tree when the priest came in.

The boy had fallen into the river, he told us. He'd been washed up on a mud bank. He must have been out walking, maybe stumbled in the dark.

"You weren't there, Father?" I said.

"Me?"

"There was no priest there, Father?"

He spread his hands. How could there have been? But he saw the yearning in our eyes.

"Christopher was a good lad," he said. "He held to his faith. God will have recognized one of his own. Now let us pray for his soul."

I clenched my fists, and I begged God to hear us.

In the yard we leant together against a frosty wall. We smoked, and tried to imagine drowning all alone in the filthy Tyne, tried to imagine what waited afterward.

"It's all ballocks," said Nixon at last.

"Eh?" we said.

"That novena stuff. It's just made up, man."

"Not just that," I said. "It's *all* made up. Every last little bit."

"Aye!" we said. "All of it. It's ballocks!"

We coughed and laughed and our breath swirled around us in the icy air. But we shuddered with the dread of what we might have done to Link, and to ourselves.

I've told nobody till now what happened next. I've tried forgetting it, I've tried not believing it, but there's been no escape.

Link came back, not long after that Christmas. I was in bed. I woke up in the middle of the night and there he was. He was standing over me, showing the massive distended bones and muscles of his arms, just like he had in the yard that day.

"It's stopped getting worse," he said. His voice was still all slobbery. "And there's no pain, and no fear."

I could smell the river on him.

"Did you jump?" I said.

He smiled.

"You could've saved me," he said. "You know that, don't you?"

"I?" I said.

"Aye. In the alleyway that day. You could've spoken up. But you didn't. You just looked away."

"Did you jump?" I said again.

He laughed and nodded.

"Yes. I did. I couldn't stand it any more so I jumped."

"Suicide," I whispered.

"Aye. Suicide."

Suicide. It was despair, a mortal sin. There could be no forgiveness. It meant eternal damnation.

I heard Hell's gates creaking open for both of us.

"So you're in Hell?" I whispered.

He smiled again.

"Because I jumped? No, that's all ballocks, just like First Fridays, novenas, all that stuff. All that matters is goodness, just simple goodness."

"And how d'you get that?"

He shrugged. He was so free, so easy, not like the Link I used to know.

"Dunno. But it seems I had it."

Then he shrugged again and he was gone.

He's kept on coming back, through all the years between. It's always the same: the smell of the river, the smile. He hasn't spoken again. Doesn't need to, I suppose. He said it all that very first time. He just stands there in the darkness, like he simply wants me to look upon him. And I do. Sometimes there's been years between his visits and I get to hope it's all over, but then he appears again, unexpected but expected, like last night. He disappeared as dawn came and then I started writing it all down at last.

It was long ago. Link's mum died soon after him.

We grammar school boys are all scattered. Some of us could well be dead. Most of us have forgotten Link, I'm sure. Nixon's ended up in California, surfing, playing golf, and drinking. He sends me cards and says it's Paradise. Me, I've always talked of moving, but I keep on staying here. Funny, but the faith draws you back, even when you don't believe it. I've gone back to lighting candles, saying my prayers in nines. I try to keep in a state of grace. I'm even in the middle of a First Friday Novena. It's all because the end's not too far away, of course.

Mebbe after that I'll discover what simple goodness is.

I hope I don't.

A story is a journey. Every word is a footstep. Every sentence, paragraph and page carries you a little further. You might know where it starts and where it's headed, but you can never be certain if you'll take the right turnings, or what you'll see and who you'll meet along the way. And, of course, a story is a life.

This story's inspired by the Great North Run, the half-marathon that takes place every year in the northeast of England. It starts in Newcastle, goes through Gateshead, Felling, Hebburn, Jarrow, and ends at South Shields, beside the North Sea. Famous athletes like Mo Farah and Paula Radcliffe take part. So do joggers and sports-club members, and people dressed as ducks and fairies. I went to the same school as Brendan Foster, the man who helped to set it all up. In Felling we lived next door to Brendan's coach, Stan Long, who started training runners when he was a welder in Gateshead. He was still Brendan's coach when Brendan became an Olympic medalist and world record holder. The Great North Run started in 1981 and it grows bigger and more famous every year. Probably influenced by Brendan and Stan, I've run it three times myself.

To prepare to write this story, I went to watch the run, of course. That morning I'd arranged to give a writing workshop in Low Newton women's prison in Durham, along with the writers Wendy Robertson and Avril Joy, who ran the educational program there. When I arrived, I was guided through a series of gates and doors by a uniformed prison officer. Each one was unlocked, opened, then shut and locked again. Keys jangled and steel clanged. I was taken to a library room with a few armchairs and tables in it. Then the women came in. They were shy at first, maybe suspicious, but they soon relaxed. I talked about my life and my writing. We did a couple of quick imagination exercises, made a few first scribbles. Some of the women began to tell me about their own lives and childhoods. They hinted at the difficulties, deprivations, and abuses they'd endured. They talked about the constrictions of being in this place, about the fellowship they tried to develop with each other, and the inevitable frictions and fights. Many of them wanted to write about themselves, to somehow turn their lives into coherent stories. I said that fictionalizing a life can make it seem more real, and can make difficult personal experiences more bearable. We scribbled again, and began to shape the scribbles into narratives.

Before I left, one of the women suddenly said, "I'm like you, David. My childhood was like yours."

She laughed.

"And look where I've ended up!" she said.

I was led back through the clanging doors. At the exit Avril told me that there was much more the women could have said.

"They've had some awful journeys," she said.

I drove away from the prison toward Felling. I parked the car. There were crowds lining the bypass, closed to traffic on this special race day. I was early. I walked down into the pebble-dashed estate where I'd spent my boyhood. I stood before the little house in which Mam, Dad, Colin, Catherine, Barbara, and I had lived, and in which Barbara had died. I watched the memories and imaginings rise for a few moments in my mind. Then I hurried back to the road.

Here came the runners, streaming past toward the sea, hundreds upon hundreds of them, sprinting, trotting, striding, dancing, exulting in their freedom, running for their lives.

Later, at home, I started to doodle a map of the route. I scribbled a few possibilities. Then the young narrator came into my mind, and he led me to Harry Miller, and both of them began to run, taking the story all the way to South Shields and back again.

harry miller's run

I don't want to go to Harry Miller's. It's Saturday morning. My entry for the Junior Great North Run's just come through the post. I'm already wearing the T-shirt. I'm already imagining belting round the quayside and over the bridges in two weeks' time. I'm imagining all the running kids, the cheering crowds. I'm dreaming of sprinting to the finish line. I phone Jacksie and we end up yelling and laughing at each other. His stuff's come as well. He's number 2594. I'm

2593. We can't believe it. But we say it's fate. We've been best mates forever. We say we'll meet up straight away and get some training done in Jesmond Dene.

But soon as I put the phone down, Mam's at my shoulder.

"Don't go," she says.

"Eh?"

"Come with me to Harry's. It's his last day in the house. He'll need a friendly face around."

"But, Mam!"

"Come on, just an hour or two. Just for me."

"But I haven't got time, Mam."

She laughs.

"You're eleven years old. You've got all the time in the world."

So in the end I sigh, phone Jacksie again and put him off till the afternoon, and I slouch down the street with my mam.

Harry's ancient. We've known him forever. He lives at the end of our street and he was fit as a lop till the heart attack got him. It looked like the end but he was soon fighting back. A few days in intensive care, a couple of weeks in Freeman Hospital, and before we knew it he was back home in Blenkinsop Street. He started tottering around his little front garden on his walker, tottering past our window to the Elmfield Social Club. He stood gasping at street corners, grinning at the neighbors, waving at the kids. When he saw me out training, he'd yell, "Gan on, young'n! Keep them pins moving!" And I'd wave and laugh and put a sprint on. "That's reet, lad! Run! There's a wolf at your tail! Run for your life!"

Everybody knows Harry. Everybody loves him. The women in the street take him flasks of tea and sandwiches and plates of dinner. His mates from the club call in with bottles of beer to play cards and dominoes with him. The district nurse visits every day and she's always laughing when she comes out his front door. But one day she found him with a massive bruise on his head after he'd had a fall. One day he was out wandering the street in his stripy pajamas. It couldn't go on. There was nobody at home to look after him. It was time for him to leave the house, get rid of tons of stuff, and move into St. Mary's, the new nursing home just off Baker's Lane.

Mam took it on herself to help him clear out. "Poor soul," she said. "How on earth'll he bear up?" But

Harry didn't seem to find it hard at all. Out went all his stuff, to charity shops and fetes and the town dump: pots and pans, dishes, tables and chairs, clothes, a radio, an ancient TV.

"What are they?" he said. "Nowt but things. Hoy them oot!"

He just laughed about it all.

"I'll not need much in the place where I'm gannin'. And for the place past that, I'll not need nowt at all."

We walk down the street to Harry's. Mam lets us in with a key. By now, just about everything's gone. The floors are bare. There're no curtains at the windows. He's sitting in the front room in a great big armchair with a box full of papers on his lap and the walker standing in front of him. There's a little table with boxes of tablets on it. He looks all dreamy but he manages to grin.

"How do, petal," he says.

"How do, Harry."

Mam bends down and kisses him. She pushes some hair back from his brow. She says has he washed this morning, has he brushed his teeth, has he had breakfast, has he . . .

"Aye," he says. "Aye, hinny, aye."

He stares at me like he's staring from a million miles away.

"It's the little runner," he says at last.

"Aye, Mr. Miller."

He reaches out and touches the T-shirt. His hand's all frail an' trembly.

"Great North Run?" he says.

"Aye, Mr. Miller."

"I done that."

"Did you really, Harry?" says Mam. "And when was that?"

He reaches toward me again.

"How old are ye, son?"

"Eleven."

"That was when I done it. When I was eleven."

Mam smiles sadly at me.

"Must've been great," she says.

"It was bliddy marvellous, pet."

He closes his eyes. Mam lifts the box from his lap. It looks like he might be dropping off to sleep, but he jumps up to his feet and grabs the walker. He leans forward like he's ready to run.

"It's the final sprint!" he says.

He giggles and drops back into the chair.

"Tek nae notice, son," he says. "I'm just a daft old maddled gadgie."

He looks at the box.

"Them'll need to be gone through," he says. "Ye'll help us, hinny?"

"'Course I will," said Mam.

He sighs and grins, and stares past us like he can see right through the walls.

"I can see the sea, mates!" he says. "We're nearly there!"

And he falls asleep and starts to snore.

It smells of old bloke in here. Suppose it's bound to. Suppose he can't help it. Suppose I'll smell like old bloke myself one day. Pee and sweat and ancient clothes and dust. The sun shines through the window. Dust's glittering and dancing in the shafts of light. Outside there're the little trees in Harry's neat little garden, the rooftops of the street, Newcastle's towers and spires, then the big blue empty sky.

Mam lifts the papers out. She unfolds them from packets and envelopes while Harry snuffles and snores.

Here's his birth certificate.

Harold Matthew Miller
Born in 1927

Father:	*Harold, a turner*
Mother:	*Maisie, a housewife*
Address:	*17 Blenkinsop Street,* *Newcastle-upon-Tyne*

"Same address as now," I say.

"Aye. Lived here all his life. And look, this must be them."

It's a small faded black-and-white photograph. A young couple and a wrapped-up baby beaming through the years. Mam holds the photograph close to Harry's face. "Can you see them in him?" she says. And when we look at Harry and think of him with his wide and shining eyes, we have to say we can. The baby, the woman and the man are living on in the sleeping bloke.

More photographs: toddler Harry in a fat nappy with his dad in overalls on one side, Mam in a flowery frock on the other. Scruffy boys and girls on benches

105

in an ancient schoolyard. A teacher at the center with a big hooked nose and a fur wrap around her shoulders. Which one is he? We pick the same face, the grinning kid just behind the teacher's head, the one lifting his hand like he wants to wave at us from seventy years ago. A final school report from 1942.

Harry is a fine hard-working lad.
We wish him well in his chosen workplace

There's his apprenticeship papers from the same year, when he started as an apprentice welder at Swan Hunter's shipyard. A photograph of him in a soldier's uniform. National service, says Mam. Harry with girls, one pretty girl then another, then another. They're on Tynemouth seafront, on Newcastle quayside market, sitting in a Ferris wheel at a fair. There's a folded piece of pink paper with a handwritten note:

Thank you, Harry. Such a lovely day.
Until next time.   Love, V

"V?" I say.

Mam shrugs.

"Who knows? I heard tell he'd been a ladies' man. Often chased but never caught."

She holds the photos to his face again.

"And there's still the handsome lad in him!" she says.

Then there he is in color, in swimming trunks and with a sombrero on his head. He's linking arms with his mates on a beach in what Mam says must be Spain.

"That's Tommy Lind!" says Mam. "And Alex Marsh, God rest his soul."

There's more, and more. Photographs and documents, savings books, rent books, pension books. There's his dad's death certificate in 1954, then his mother's just a few months later, both of them with cancer, both of them too young. There're holiday bookings, airline tickets, outdated foreign money. Lists of medication, prescriptions, hospital appointment cards.

"A whole life in a box," says Mam as she lifts another envelope and opens it. "What's this?" she says to herself.

"It's what I telt ye," says Harry. He's wide awake. "It's the Great North bliddy Run."

There're four skinny kids on a beach, three lads and a lass. The sun's blazing down. The lads are wearing baggy shorts and boots, and they've got vests slung over their bare shoulders. The lass is in a white dress and she's wearing boots as well. They're all grinning and holding massive ice creams in their fists.

"Pick us out," says Harry.

We both point to the same lad.

"That's reet," he says. "And that one's Norman Wilkinson, and he was Stanley Swift." He pauses as he looks. He touches the girl's face and smiles. "She joined us at Felling. Veronica was her name."

He grins.

"It was took by Angelo Gabrieli, the ice-cream maker."

He keeps on grinning.

"It's South Shields," he says.

"South Shields?" says Mam.

"Look, there's the pier in the haze. There's Tynemouth Castle in the distance."

We peer closely.

"Oh, aye," we say.

"We run there from Newcastle," says Harry.

We just look at him.

"We were eleven years old," he says. "It was 1938. We were young and daft and fit as fleas."

He points to the envelope.

"Keep digging, hinny."

She takes out a sheet of paper. It crackles as she

unfolds it. It's faded at the edges. The writing's all discolored. Mam reads it out.

THIS IS TO SERTIFY THAT

Harold Matthew Miller

RUN FROM NEWCASLE TO SOUTH SHIELDS ON
29 AUGUST 1938.

What a grate achevemente!
GOOD LAD! WEL DONE!

SINED

Angelo Gabrieli

MASTER ICE-CREAM MAKER OF SOUTH SHIELDS
29 AUGUST 1938

"He made one for all of us," says Harry. "And he sent the photographs to all of us."

We don't know what to say. He laughs at us.

"It's true," he says. "It was a lovely summer's day. Norman says, 'I'd love a swim.' So Stanley says, 'Let's go to Shields.'"

"But Harry . . ." says Mam.

He points to the envelope.

"And we got our swim," he says.

Another photograph. The same kids, in the sea this time, yelling with laughter as the breakers roll over them.

"Beautiful," he murmurs. "We were that hot and sweaty and fit to drop, and it was wet and icy and tingly and just that lovely. And Mr. Gabrieli with the camera. Can see him still, standing in the sunlight, laughing and urging us on. Dark hair and dark eyes and broad shoulders and dressed in white. A lovely man."

"But it's thirteen miles," says Mam.

He sighs, he leans back in his chair. "Giz a minute. Any chance of a cup of tea?" She makes it. It trembles as he lifts it to his lips. He drinks. He drinks again. "Lovely cup of tea," he says. "One of them tablets. Aye, the white ones, love." He takes the tablet, he drinks more tea. He blinks, takes a breath. "Thirteen miles. We weren't to know. Stanley said he went there with his Uncle Jackie on the train one day. Said it was just across the Tyne Bridge then through a place called Felling then turn left and a short bit more. Said it'd mebbe take an hour at most and we'd be back for tea." He giggles. "We didn't do geography at school, except to find out aboot Eskimos and pygmies and the River Nile."

"But what did you tell your mams?" says Mam.

"Nowt! Nowt at all." He looks at me. "We were

always shooting off to the town moor or Exhibition Park, or just pottering around the streets and lanes. They were used to us going out in the morning and not coming back till nearly dark. Don't believe it, de ye?"

"Dunno," I say.

"Different days, son. Mind you, by the time we got to Felling, we were starting to see what we'd took on."

He drinks some more tea.

"We started at ten o'clock. It was already hot. Stanley said, 'Just think of that icy watter on your skin, lads.' So we belted out of Blenkinsop Street and down to the bridge. What a clatter! All of us had studs in our boots that our dads'd hammered in te mek them last longer. We started off by racing each other, but after a while I said, 'Tek it easy, man, lads. No need for racing yet.'" He looked at me. "You'll understand that, eh? Save some breath for the final sprint?"

"Aye, Mr. Miller," I say.

"Aye. Good lad." He looks at my T-shirt again. "It's not the full run ye'll be diying, is it?"

"No," I say. "Just the junior one. A couple of miles around the bridges and the quay. You've got to be seventeen to do the proper Great North Run."

"Seventeen. So we were even dafter than I thought.

Anyway, we trotted across the bridge and there were ships lined up along the river underneath, and seagulls screaming all around, and lots of folk walking on the bridge that we had to dodge past. We get to Gateshead and onto the High Street and we ask a fruiterer if we can have a drink of watter, please, cos we're running to South Shields today. 'To South bliddy Shields?' he says. 'You better have some apples an' all. Are ye sure?' he sez. 'Aye,' we say. 'It's just roond the corner, isn't it?' 'Depends what ye mean by roond the corner,' he says. We just laugh and take the apples and run on cos we're still full o' beans and it's great to be together on a summer's day. Then there's Sunderland Road that gets us to Felling, and it's a lang straight road and we've already been gannin' for nearly an hour. There's no sign of any sea, no end in sight. And we sit doon by Felling railway station and we look at each other and nobody says a word till Norman says at last, 'So where the hell's South Shields?' Stanley points along the road. 'That way, I think,' he says. 'I divent knaa exactly, but I'm certain we're gannin' the reet way.' Norman just looks at him. 'I'm getting knackered,' he says. 'Let's gan back.' And probly we would have. But then we seen her, across the street, lookin' doon at us."

"Who?" says Mam.

"Veronica."

He sips his tea again. He sighs and blows.

"You knaa," he says. "It comes to something when talking aboot runnin' gets as knackerin' as runnin' itself." He grins. "Divent get old, son. Promise us that. Stay eleven forever."

"OK, Mr. Miller," I say.

"Good lad. I bet you're fast, are ye?"

"Not that fast. I can keep going, though."

"Ye'd have been good that day, then. And ye'll be all set when you're seventeen."

"Aye. I think I will."

"Just wait till ye see that sea, shining before ye after all them miles."

"Veronica, Harry," says Mam.

"Eh?" says Harry.

"Veronica. Who was she?"

"Veronica? She was something else."

He turns his face to the ceiling. He closes his eyes like he's imagining it all again, then he opens them again and there's such a smile on his face.

"She was on the green at the end of a row of terraced houses," he says. "She was hanging washing oot. She stopped what she was diyin' and she had one hand up across her eyes to shade them from the sun. 'Gan and ask her for some watter,' sez Norman. 'Gan yourself,' sez Stanley. 'I'll gan,' sez I. And off I go. I can see her now, standing in her white cotton dress with the basket of washing under her arm and the way she watches us as I get closer. 'What do you want?' she sez when I get closer. 'Is there any chance of a cup of watter?' I say. 'We've been runnin' from Newcastle and we're parched.' 'From Newcastle?' she sez. 'Aye,' I say. 'From Blenkinsop Street. We were ganna run te South Shields but I think we're turning back.' 'Why's that?' she sez. 'Cos we're knackered,' I say. 'And South Shields is a lang way. And to be honest we divent really knaa where it is.' She puts the washing doon. 'Turning back?' she sez. 'And you don't even know where it is? What kind of attitude is that?' 'I divent knaa,' I say. 'But if you'll be kind enough to give us some watter we'll be on our way.' And she sez, 'Wait there,' and she turns round and walks away."

He says nothing for a while. It looks like he's going all dreamy again, like he might doze off again.

"Did she bring some water?" says Mam.

"Eh? Aye, she did. A big bottle of it. And she's got

jam sandwiches an' all, and she's got big boots on and she sez, 'There's no need to turn back. I know where South Shields is. I've left a note for my mother. I'll take you there.' And she puts a sandwich in me hand, and walks down to where the other two is. She tells them an' all while they're eating the sandwiches and swigging the watter. 'But we're half knackered already,' sez Stanley. 'By the time we run aal the way back again we'll be bliddy deed.' 'There's no need to run back again,' she sez. 'We can take the train. You'll be back for tea.' And when we start to laugh she goes into the pocket in her dress and takes some money out. 'I'll pay,' she sez. 'My Uncle Donald sends it to me. He lives in America. He says he works in Hollywood. I think he's fibbing but that doesn't matter.' Me and the lads look at each other. A train steams through the station. I look at her, I think of the train, I taste the lovely bread and jam, and I swig the lovely watter. 'I'm Veronica,' says Veronica. 'What're your names?' So we tell her, and so she says, 'What we waiting for?' She smiles her smile at me. Me and the lads look at each other. 'Nowt,' I say. 'Nowt,' say the other two. 'This way, then,' she sez, and we set off running again."

"Quite a girl," says Mam.

"Aye," says Harry.

He goes silent again. Mam says does he want more tea. He says yes. She goes to make it. I look at my watch, I think about Jacksie, I think about running through Jesmond Dene.

"Things to do?" says Harry.

"Aye."

He nods. "I'll not be lang. I cannot be. Or like Stanley said, by the time I finish I'll be bliddy dead. More tea. Good lass! Ha, and a slice of jam and bread and all!"

Mam smiles with him.

"Eat it up," she says. "It'll give you strength."

And he eats, and wipes his lips with his shaky hand, and after a moment he starts again.

"So we run out of Felling and down through Pelaw and Bill Quay and into Hebburn, and it's getting hot as Hell and staying bright as Heaven. And Veronica runs smooth and free beside us. And our feet clatter and beat on the tracks and pavements, and sometimes we walk and rest and gather our breath and run again. And sometimes we shout out to folks we pass that we're running to South Shields and we've run from Blenkinsop Street in Newcastle and from Felling station and they say they don't believe it. They say it's such a bliddy wonder! 'Good lads!' they say. 'Good lass! Run! Run! There's a wolf at your tail! Run for your lives!' And people give us watter, and a baker in Hebburn gives us cakes. And we run and run and run and run. And we get to Jarrow and we rest in the shade under the trees in St. John's churchyard, and we watch a coffin bein' carried from a hearse through a group of mourners and put into the ground, and out of the blue Veronica stretches her arms out wide and says, 'They said I might not live at all. And just look what I can do!'"

"How do you mean?" says Mam.

"That's what I sez—'How d'you mean?' Veronica shrugs. 'I was a weakly child,' she says. 'I was back and forward to the doors of death.' Me and the lads is hushed. They were different days back then. There were many little'ns took too soon. Stanley hisself had a sister gone before he was born. 'Are you all right now?' he whispers to Veronica. And she laughs, the way she did. 'Now how could I run to South Shields if I wasn't, Stanley?' And up she jumps with her big heart and her big soul and her strong legs and her big boots and we're off again, and as we leave Jarrow behind we start telling each other we can smell the sea. Which was more a matter of hope than truth. Nae sign of any sea. Nae sign of any South Shields. We've soon been gone more than two hours. It's afternoon. It's blazin' hot. We're absolutely knacked. We're slowin' doon. Nobody says it but we're all thinking of giving up. Even Veronica starts puffin' and pantin' and gaspin' for air, and Stanley's watching her with great concern. And then we hear it, the clip-clop-clip of Gabrieli's pony and the toot of Gabrieli's horn." He laughs at the memory. "It come upon us like a miracle."

"The ice-cream maker?" says Mam.

"Aye. Mr. Angelo Gabrieli, master ice-cream maker of South Shields. He's on an ice-cream cart that's painted all white and red and gold. The pony's shining black. Mr. Gabrieli's sitting there in his white shirt and his white trousers and his white cap with **GABRIELI'S** printed on it and there's a great big tub of ice cream at his side. He toots his horn again. He laughs. 'Buy a Gabrieli!' he calls. 'Best ice cream this side of Heaven!' And he tugs the pony to a halt at our side. We halt as well. We puff and pant. We drool. We watch the shining tub. I think of Veronica's cash. Never mind the train, I think. Buy some ice creams now! 'Good afternoon, my fine children!' says Mr. Gabrieli. 'And where might you be going on this perfect day?' 'South

118

Shields,' I tell him. He grins in satisfaction. 'The perfect destination! Your names, my friends?' We tell him our names. I tell him we've run all the way from Newcastle and Felling. 'Indeed?' he says. 'I thought you looked a little hot. Perhaps a little ice cream would be rather helpful.' We daren't speak. We look at Veronica. Our eyes and hearts are yearning. 'Perhaps a little one now,' says Mr. Gabrieli, 'and the biggest one you've ever seen when at last you reach the beach!' And he opens the tub and digs into it, and gives us each an ice cream for free. Ha! And nothing I've tasted in the seventy years since has tasted anything like that glorious gift. Mr. Gabrieli smiles as he watches us. He ponders. 'I could offer you a lift,' he says, and Norman's mouth is opening wide with joy. But Veronica's shaking her head and telling him no. 'Yes, you are right, Veronica,' says Mr. Gabrieli. 'This is an achievement you will remember all your lives. Do not worry, boys. It is not far now. Along here then right and onto lovely Ocean Road, and then at the end of that—the shining sea itself! I will meet you there!' He snaps the reins. 'Onward, Francisco! Until we meet again, my friends!' And off he trots."

Harry rests. He gazes out at the trees and the sky. Mam brings more tea.

"You've not told anybody about this till now?" she says.

"I've told bits of it, pet, just like bits of crack and reminiscing at the club. But I've never telt it all with all the detail in. And even now, there'll be bits of it I must leave out."

"It was such an amazing thing, Harry," Mam says. "Like Mr. Gabrieli said, such a great achievement."

"Aye, that's true. And it was a day of daftness and joy, and if we'd never started and we'd never kept on going, just think of what we'd've missed." He smiles, like he's slipping into a dream. "So we kept on going and we kept on going. We followed Gabrieli's cart until it went right out of sight, and we kept on going with the lovely thought of massive ice creams still to come. And then we're on Ocean Road, and there's seagulls in the air and a breeze on our faces, and this time we can truly smell the sea, and then, 'Oh, I can see it, mates! I can really see the sea!'"

And Harry's eyes are wide, like he can see the sea again.

"And he's there, like he said he would be. Mr. Gabrieli. He's sitting up on his cart and he smiles to welcome us and holds his arms out wide. 'Now,' he says. 'Which should come first? The ice cream or the sea?' And we divent hesitate. We're straight onto the beach and plunging into the watter. And when we look back, there's Mr. Gabrieli laughing at us as we jump and dive and tumble through the waves. Then we stand together and he photographs us, and we come out and he leads us to the cart and he gives us the biggest ice creams we've ever seen, then he photographs us again. And he has our certificates ready and we sit in the sand and read them to each other. And then Mr. Gabrieli asks us if we know that we are wonderful, and he sings to us — something I never heard before and have never heard since, except in dreams, something Italian and strange and very beautiful."

He points to the envelope.

"Should be something else in there," he says. "He got some passerby to take it."

Mam slips her fingers inside and takes it out, another photograph. Everybody's in it, standing smiling before the ice-cream cart and Francisco the shining pony. Harry, Veronica, Stanley, and Norman with their certificates, and lovely Mr. Gabrieli himself, all in white with **GABRIELI'S** printed on his cap, and past them is the beach and then the sea. And me and Mam don't say anything, though we can see that Harry and Veronica are standing right together, holding hands.

"And then," says Harry, "we give our addresses to Mr. Gabrieli and we say good-bye. And back we go up Ocean Road and to the railway station. And then we get the train, and off it puffs, through Jarrow and Hebburn and Pelaw and Heworth, doing in minutes what took us so long. And then along the track to Felling."

"And Veronica?" says Mam.

"She got off there. And we went on. And we were home in time for tea."

"You know what I mean. Did you see her again?"

"Most nights, in me dreams."

"No more than that?"

He shakes his head, closes his eyes, then points into the box.

"That brown packet there," he says.

She lifts it out.

"Gan on," he says.

She opens it, and there they are, Harry and Veronica. They're on the Tyne Bridge, maybe eighteen years old. The breeze is in their hair and there're seagulls in the air behind them, and they're laughing out loud and holding hands again.

"Aye," he says. He takes the photograph and holds it. "We made sure we found each other again. And we were together for a time. And she really was something else. But then . . ."

His voice falters. He shakes his head.

"Not now, love. I'm knacked. The lad's got running to do, I've got a home to go to, and you've got some helping out to do."

"OK then, Harry," says Mam.

She kisses him. She tells him to close his eyes, to have a rest.

"Aye, I will," he says. He licks his lips and stares into the photograph.

"Do you think . . . ?" he says to Mam.

"Think what, Harry?"

"Do you think there's a Heaven, like they used to say there was? A Heaven where we meet again?"

"I don't know, Harry."

"Me neither. And mebbe it doesn't matter. Mebbe this is Heaven. Mebbe you enter Heaven on the best of days, like the day we got to Shields, like other days."

"Days with her? With Veronica?"

"Aye. Days with Veronica."

His eyes flutter. He looks at me.

"You're a good lad. Get started, keep on going. You'll have a lovely life."

He closes his eyes.

"You know what?" he murmurs before he sleeps. "Me great achievement is that I've been happy, that I've never been nowt but happy."

"Go on, son," says Mam. "Go and see Jacksie. Get your training in."

Harry never got to St. Mary's Nursing Home. He died that afternoon while I was running with Jacksie through Jesmond Dene. Mam said he just slipped away like he was going into a deeper sleep. She arranged the funeral. People came to our house afterward. We played a CD of Italian songs. There was beer and a big tub of ice cream, and there was crying, and lots and lots of laughter. I ran again that afternoon with Jacksie, and I heard Harry deep inside me: "That's reet, lad! Run! There's a wolf at your tail! Run for your lovely life!"

A week later we ran the Junior Great North Run. We belted round the quayside and across the bridges, hundreds of us running through the sunlight by the glittering river and through the cheering crowds. We raced each other to the finish line, me an' my best mate Jacksie, numbers 2593 and 2594, and Jacksie just got there in front of me. It didn't matter. We stood arm in arm with our medals and certificates. We laughed into Mam's camera. We were young and daft. We'd run the run, and we felt so free and light I really thought we might have run into a bit of Heaven.

Next day she drove us all to Felling. We stood on the bypass and here they came, the thin, fast lines of professionals and champions and record-holders and harriers; then the others—hundreds after hundreds after hundreds of them—puffing and panting, grinning and gasping. Here came the young and the old, the determined and the barmy. They waved and grimaced and sighed and giggled. They squirted water over their heads and over us. There were gorillas and ducks and Supermans and bishops and Frankensteins and Draculas and nurses. And the watchers laughed and yelled.

"You're doing great!" yelled Mam. "Good lad! Good lass! Gan on! Well done!"

And then I saw them. They were kids, too little and young for this run. Three skinny lads in vests and boots that thudded on the road, a dark-haired lass in boots as well and wearing a white dress. They twisted and dodged and threaded their way through the crowd. And I looked at Mam a moment, and her eyes were wide with astonishment and wonder as well. As the four of them passed by, one of the lads lifted his hand high and waved at us and laughed, and then was off again. And they'd gone, lost again in the crowd, a crowd that kept on running past and running past, a crowd we couldn't wait to join, a crowd that seemed like the whole of Tyneside, the whole of the world, all running through the blazing sunlight to the sea.

Sometimes, usually in winter, I get to wondering, why on earth do I live in the north? It gets so cold! It seems so far away from everywhere! Then I go to the coast, and I start to understand again. As a kid I used to stand at the top of the town and look down to the river, snaking its way past shipyards, warehouses, great cranes, the cluttered riverbanks of Hebburn, Jarrow, Tyne Dock, then flowing between the twin piers at Tynemouth and South Shields to merge with the North Sea. Sometimes the sea shone brilliant blue and sometimes it was almost black. When the wind was right, you could smell it. Seagulls squawked above our streets. When there was fog, the river bells rang, and distant foghorns droned. The lights of ships shone at night like stars. The sea was always with us, part of what we were, and it seemed we always wanted to be near to it.

On bright Sundays our family went on car trips to South Shields. There's a photograph of us all — we've put up a windbreak and spread our blankets on the sand, and the beach all around is packed with folk. Granddad's there, a huge, round, silent man, in his blue serge three-piece suit, his cloth cap, his big black boots, sitting with his legs straight out, puffing on his pipe as always. Grandma, almost as big as he is, in her floral frock, pours tea from a thermos. Dad's still got his glasses on, wearing his green trunks, hands on hips, poised for action. Three kids: Colin, Catherine, me, all in swimming gear. Mam's wrapped up in a cardigan and scarf because of her arthritis. I can hear her words.

"Go on. Run and play. Those that can run should run, those that can play should play."

Soon we'll wade into the water, dive and swim furiously out against the waves. Yes, it'll be bitterly cold, but so what? You quickly get used to it. And yes, we'll shudder and our knees will knock when we run back out again, but Dad'll wrap towels around us and rub us hard to get us warm. And there'll be hot tea, and fish and chips from Frankie's. We'll be in and out of the water all day long, just like dozens of other kids all along the beach. Back then I thought that all seas must be the same. I recall my amazement when I swam in the Mediterranean for the first time.

The best trips took us farther. We'd drive north, up the Great North Road and across the Great Northern Coalfield, where pitheads still filled the landscape and men in their thousands still worked underground. We headed to what lay beyond: the beaches and sea villages of Northumberland; Craster, Embleton, Beadnell. These were wild and lovely places: long, pale beaches with rolling dunes behind; the Farne Islands stretching toward the horizon; the ruined castle of Dunstanburgh on its rocky black headland; Bamburgh Castle, high above its village and its beach; Lindisfarne Castle like a mirage way out on its long, low island; distant lighthouses. Everything was on a greater scale: a sea so wide you could see the curve of the earth upon it; the Cheviot Hills rising darkly above the land behind; families scattered sparsely across the great sweeps of sand. Flights of puffins dashed over us, terns danced above the waves, oystercatchers picked at the shore, gannets plunged from on high.

And there were seals, and sometimes dolphins and porpoises, that rolled in the water's surge.

Mam sat in a deckchair unwrapping our picnic while we played war games in the dunes with Dad. On the days I recall, the younger children were now with us: Barbara, who so quickly disappeared, then Mary and Margaret. We lit driftwood fires. We built castles from damp sand and from the weird objects thrown up by the sea. We played in the rock pools, turning stones to find crabs below. And we swam and swam, then took the long drive home again, sleeping and dreaming as we headed back toward Tyneside's light.

As I grew older, I left family trips behind. And Dad died, so the trips were no longer possible anyway. But I still went there with my friends. We took the slow bus from Newcastle, or we hitchhiked in pairs. Sometimes we took tents and pitched them at the small duneside site in Beadnell or at Waren Mill beyond Bamburgh. Sometimes we slept in bus shelters or under fishing boats or in soft hollows in the dunes. We took loaves of bread and tins of Spam and hunks of cheese. We had bonfires and beach parties. We swam in the shallow waters of Beadnell

Bay while the sun went down over the Cheviots and the sea and sky glowed pink and gold. I fell in love for the first time on Beadnell Beach — with an eighteen-year-old art student. I was fifteen. She must have been humoring me, but we sat by the embers deep into the night. We watched the rays of Longstone Lighthouse sweeping across the sea, the land, the sea again. We talked about the beauty of the moon, gasped in wonder at the stars and at this world, and I gazed at her as the light passed over, and imagined she must be some lovely creature from the sea itself.

I still go there as often as I can, to walk the beaches in that intensely clear air and light. I wade in the water (I don't swim — I understand now how stunningly cold the water is!). I sometimes go there to write, and even when I'm not writing, the words are somehow always there, part of the geography of my imagination.

Stupor Beach, the village in the story, isn't a real place. It exists in a fictional Northumberland — it's a little like Boulmer or Newton or Alnmouth. The girl who tells the tale lives in a version of the wooden shacks that still exist in the dunes around those places. They're beautiful, much-loved rickety creations, built decades ago as holiday homes by long-gone pitmen.

Annie loves the place where she lives. She knows that somehow her true identity comes from the sea.

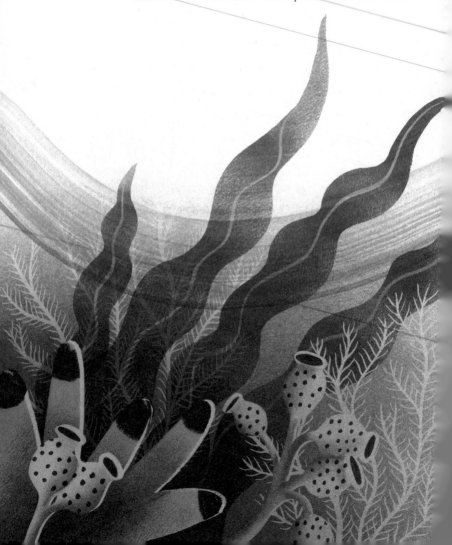

half a creature from the sea

My mother says that all things can be turned to tales. When she said it first I thought she meant tales like fish tails, but I was wrong. She meant tales like this, tales that are stories. But this tale of mine is very like a fish tail too.

This is about me and my mum, and where we come from. And it's about the man who came one sunlit day and took the picture that hangs on the wall by my bed and shows the truth of me. His name was Benn. So this little tale of mine is some of his tale too.

I'm Annie Lumsden and I live with my mum in a

house above the jetsam line on Stupor Beach. I'm thirteen years old and growing fast. I have hair that drifts like seaweed when I swim. I have eyes that shine like rock pools. My ears are like scallop shells. The ripples on my skin are like the ripples on the sand when the tide has turned back again. At night I gleam and glow like the sea beneath the stars and moon. Thoughts dart and dance inside like little minnows in the shallows. They race and flash like mackerel farther out. My wonderings roll in the deep like seals. Dreams dive each night into the dark like dolphins do, and break out happy and free into the morning light. These are the things I know about myself and that I see when I look in the rock pools at myself. They are the things that I see when I look at the picture the man from America give to me before he went away.

Our house is a shack and is wooden, white, and salty. We have a room each at the back with a bed each and a cupboard each and a chair each. We have a kitchen just like everybody has and a bathroom just like everybody has. From the kitchen window we can see the village past the dunes—the steeple of St. Mungo's Church, the flag on top of Stupor Primary School, the chimney pot on the Slippery Eel. At the front of the shack is the room with the big wide window that looks out across the rocks and rock pools and the turning sea toward the rocky islands. There are many tales about the islands. Saints lived on one of them long ago. Another of them has an ancient castle on a rock. It's said that mermaids used to live out there, and sing sailors to their doom. We are in the north. It is very beautiful. They say it's cold here, especially the water, but I know nothing else, so it isn't cold to me. Nor to Mum, who loves this place too. She was brought up in the city, but ever since she was a girl she knew her happiness would be found by the sea.

We have a sandy garden with a rickety fence and in the garden are patterns of seashells, and rocks that Mum has painted with lovely faces. Mum sells models made from shells—sailing ships and mermaids' thrones and fancy cottages—in the Lyttle Gyfte Shoppe next to the Slippery Eel. She sells her painted rocks there too. When I was little, I thought that these rocks were the faces of sisters and brothers and friends that had been washed up by the sea for me. This made Mum laugh.

"No, my darling, they are simply rocks."

Then she lifted one of the rocks to her face and showed how all things, even rocks that have lain forever on an ordinary beach, can be made to turn to tales.

"Hello," she whispered to this rock, which bore the face of a sweet dark-haired little boy on it.

"Hello," it whispered back in such a soft, sweet voice.

"What is your name?" Mum said.

"My name is Septimus Samuel Swift," replied the rock, and Mum held it close to her lips and let it look at me as it told its tale of being the seventh son of a seventh son and of traveling with pirates to Madagascar and fighting with sea monsters in the Sea of Japan.

"Was that you that spoke the words?" I asked.

She winked and smiled.

"How could you think such a thing?" she said.

And she stroked my hair and set off singing a sea shanty, the kind she sings on folk nights in the Slippery Eel.

She finds tales everywhere—in grains of sand she picks up from the garden, in puffs of smoke that drift out from the chimneys of the village, in fragments of smooth timber or glass in the jetsam. She will ask them, "Where did you come from? How did you get here?" And they will answer her in voices very like her own, but with new lilts and squeaks and splashes in them that show they are their own. Mum is good with tales.

Sometimes she visits Stupor Primary School and tells them to the young ones. I used to sit with the children and listen. The teachers there, Mrs. Marr and Miss Malone, were always so happy to see me again. "How are you getting on?" they asked while the children giggled and whispered, "She's dafter than ever."

Long ago, they tried me at Stupor Primary School. It didn't work. I couldn't learn. Words in books stayed stuck to the page like barnacles. They wouldn't turn themselves to sound and sense for me. Numbers clung to their books like limpets. They wouldn't add, subtract, or multiply for me. The children mocked and laughed. The teachers were gentle and kind but soon they started to shake their heads and turn away from me. They asked Mum to come in for a chat. I'd been assessed, they said. Stupor Church of England Primary School couldn't give me what I needed. There was another school in another place where there were other children like me. I stood at the window that day while they talked at my back. I looked across the fields behind the school toward the hidden city where that other place would be. It broke my heart to think that I must spend my days so distant from my mum and from the sea. "It's for the best," said Mrs. Marr. That was a momentous moment, the moment of my first fall. My legs went weak beneath me and I tumbled to the floor and the whole world went watery and dark, and wild watery voices sang sweetly in my brain and called me to them. I came out of it to find Mum weeping over me and shaking me and screaming my name like I had drifted a million miles away, and the teacher yelling for help into the phone.

I reached up and caught Mum's falling tears.

"It's all right," I whispered sweetly to her. "It was lovely, Mum."

And it was. And I wanted it to happen again. And soon it did. And did again.

There followed months of trips to hospitals and visits to doctors and many, many tries to go past my strangeness and to find the secrets and the truth in me. There were lights shone deep into my eyes, blood sucked out of me, wires fixed to me, questions asked of me. There were stares and glares and pondering and wondering, and medicines and needles, and much talk coming out of many flapping mouths, and much black writing written on much white paper. I was wired wrong. The chemicals that flowed in me were wrong. My brain was an electric storm. There had been damage from disease, from a bang on the head, damage at my birth. It ended with a single doctor, Dr. John, in a single room with Mum and me.

"There is something wrong with Annie," said Dr. John.

"Something?" asked my mum.

"Yes," said Dr. John. He scratched his head. "Something. But we don't know what the something is so we haven't got a name for it."

And we were silent. And I was very pleased. And Mum hugged me.

And Dr. John said, "All of us are mysteries, even to us white-coated doctors. And some of us are a bit more of a puzzle than the rest of us."

He smiled into my eyes. He winked.

"You're a good girl, Annie Lumsden," he said.

"She is," said Mum.

"What's the thing," said Dr. John, "that you like best in the whole wide world?"

And I answered, "My mum is that thing. That, and splashing and swimming like the fishes in the sea."

"Then that's good," he said. "For unlike most of us, you have the things you love close by you. And you have them there on little Stupor Beach. Be happy. Go home."

So we went home.

A teacher, Miss McLintock, came each Tuesday. I stayed daft.

We went back to Dr. John each six weeks or so. I stayed a puzzle.

And we walked on the beach, sat in the sandy garden. Mum painted her rocks and glued her shells, and told her tales and sang her shanties. I swam and swam, and we were happy.

"I sometimes think," I said one day, "I should have been a fish."

"A fish?"

"Aye. Sometimes I dream I've got fins and a tail."

"Goodness gracious!" said Mum.

She jumped up and lifted my T-shirt and looked at my spine.

"What's there?" I said.

She kissed me.

"Nowt, my little minnow," she said.

She looked again.

"Thank goodness for that," she said.

I fell many, many times. It happened in the salty shack, in the sandy garden, on the sandy beach. My legs would lose their strength and I would tumble, and the whole of everything would turn watery, and it was like I really turned from Annie Lumsden into something else—to a fish or a seal or a dolphin. And when the world turned back into sand and rocks and shacks and gardens, I would find Mum sitting close by, watching over me, waiting for me to return, and she'd smile and say, "Where've you been, my little swimmer?" I'd tell her I'd been far away beneath the sea to places of coral and shells and beautifully colored fish, and she'd smile and smile to hear the words loosened from my tongue as I told my traveling tales. At first, Mum was scared that I would fall and lose myself when I was in the water, and that I would drown and be taken from her, but we came to know that it did not, and would never, happen, for in the water I am truly as I am—Annie Lumsden, seal girl, fish girl, dolphin girl, the girl who cannot drown.

Then there came the sunlit day, the day of Benn. I lay on the warm sand at Mum's side. My body and brain were reforming themselves after a fall. Every time it happened, it was like being born again, like coming out from dark and lovely water and crawling into the world like a little new thing. She was gently stroking my seaweed hair, and we were lost in wonder at the puzzle of myself and the mystery of everything that is and ever was and ever will be. I gazed at her and asked, "Mum, tell me where I come from."

And she started to tell me a tale I knew so well, ever since I was a little one.

"Once," she said, "when I was walking by the sea, I saw a fisherman."

It was the old familiar tale. A man was fishing on the beach, casting his line far out into the water. A handsome man, in green waterproofs and green wellies. A hardworking man from far down south, taking a break at Stupor Beach. Mum passed by. They got to talking. He said he loved the wildness of the north. They got to drinking and dancing in the Slippery Eel. He listened to Mum singing her shanties. He called her a wild northern lass. He wasn't a bad man, not really, just a bit careless and a bit feckless. He stayed a while then quickly went away. He was searched for and never was found. Charles, his name was, or he said it was. To tell the truth, he wouldn't have made a decent daddy. It was better like this, just Mum and me.

But that day I put my finger to her lips.

"No," I told her. "Not that old one. I know that one."

"But it's true."

"Tell me something with a better truth in it, something that works out the puzzle of me."

"Turn you into a tale?"

"Aye. Turn me to a tale."

She winked.

"I didn't want to tell you this," she said. "Will you keep it secret?"

"Aye," I said.

She leant over and looked at my back and stroked my spine.

"Nowt there," she said. "But maybe it's time to tell the truth at last."

And I lay there on the sand beneath the sun, and the sea rolled and turned close by, and seagulls cried, and the breeze lifted tiny grains of sand and scattered them on me. And Mum's fingers moved on me and she breathed and sighed and her voice started to flow over me and into me as sweet as any song, and it found in me a different Annie Lumsden; an Annie Lumsden that fitted with my fallings, my dreams, my body, and the sea.

"I was swimming," she murmured. "It was summer, morning, very early—milky white sky, not a breath of wind, water like glass. Most of the world was deep asleep. Not a soul to be seen but a man in the dunes with a dog a quarter of a mile away. Nowt on the sea except a single dinghy slipping northward. Gannets high, high up and little terns darting back and forth into the water for fish, and nervy oystercatchers by the rock pools. The tide had turned, and it went back nearly soundless, just a gentle lovely hissing as it drained away; and all around, the secrets of the sea were given up—the rocks, the pools, the weeds, the darting creatures and the crawling and the scuttling creatures, the million grains of sand. And as I swam I was drawn backward and outward toward the islands, and farther from the line of jetsam and my things. Rocks began appearing all around. A great field of seaweed was exposed nearby, with stems as thick as children's arms and long brown rubbery leaves."

"Were you young?"

"Fourteen years younger than I am today. A young woman, and strong, with strong, smooth swimming muscles on my shoulders. My things were high up on the beach beyond the jetsam—a red plastic bag, a green towel laid out. I remember as I swam and dived and drifted that I felt stunned, almost hypnotized. I kept trying to look back to the red and green, to remind myself that the solid world was the world I'd come from and that I must swim back again."

She smiled at me.

"You know that feeling?"

I smiled.

"You know I know that feeling."

"And as I drifted, I felt the first touch on me."

"The touch?"

"A gentle tender touch. At first I told myself it was the shifting of the seaweed, or the flicker of a little fish fin. But then it came again, like something touching, deliberately touching. Something moved beneath. It moved right under me. A flickering swimming thing, slow and smooth. And it was gone. Then I was suddenly cold, and tiredness and hunger were in me. I stayed calm. I swam breaststroke slowly for the shore. I knelt in the wet sand there and told myself that I'd been wrong, I'd been deceived. I looked back. The sea was empty. I started to walk up the slope of wet sand toward my things. A bird screamed. I looked back again. A little tern hung dancing in the air close behind me, beak pointing down toward the water. It screamed again, then wheeled away as the man appeared from the brown-leaved weed."

"The man?" I whispered.

"He was slender, but with great shoulders on him. Hair slick like weed. Skin smooth and bright like sealskin. He crouched at the water's edge, poised between the land and sea. He cupped his hands and drank the sea. He raised his eyes toward the low milky sun and lowered them again. I could not, dared not, move. I saw the fin folded along his back."

"The fin?"

"I saw his webbed fingers, his webbed toes. His eyes were huge and dark and shining. He laughed, as if the moment brought him great joy. He cupped his hands again and poured water over himself. Then he raised his eyes and looked at me, and after a moment of great stillness in us both, he left the sea and came to me."

"You ran away?"

"There seemed no threat in him, no danger. I looked along the beach. The man with his dog in the dunes was a world away. The man with the fin came out. He knelt a yard away from me."

"Did he speak?"

"There was a sound from him, a splashing sound, like water rather than air was moving in his throat."

"What was he?"

"A mystery. A secret of the sea. He was very beautiful. I saw in his eyes he thought I was beautiful too."

I looked into my mother's eyes. What did I see there? The delight of memories or the delight of her imaginings?

"He was my father?" I whispered.

Her eyes were limpid pools.

"That was the first day," she said. "We moved no closer to each other. We did not touch. I saw the water drying on him, leaving salt on his beautiful skin. When he saw this, he lowered himself into the field of weed again and he was gone. But he came back again on other early milky mornings when the sea was calm. The last day he came, he stayed an hour with me. He came onto the land. We stayed in the shade beneath the rocks. I poured water from the rock pools over him. He was very beautiful, and his liquid voice was very beautiful."

"He was my father?"

"I touched his fin, his webs, his seaweed hair that day. I remember them still against my fingers. That last day we had to hurry back to the water. Despite the rock-pool water, his skin was drying out, his voice was coarse, his eyes were suddenly touched with dread. We ran back to the water. He sighed as he lowered himself into the water. We looked at each other, he from within the sea, I from without. He reached out of the sea to me. His hand was dripping wet, and in it was a shell—this shell."

She opened her palm. In it was a seashell.

"Then he swam away."

I took the shell from her. It was as ordinary as any seashell, as beautiful as any seashell.

"I'll cut the story short," she said. "Nine months later you were born."

"And it's true?"

"And yes, it's—"

We heard a click. We turned. A man was standing close by. He held a camera to his face. He lowered it.

"Forgive me," he said.

He moved toward us.

"But you were so lovely, the two of you there. It was just like the girl had been washed up by the sea."

We said nothing, were still lost in the tale that Mum had told.

"Name's Benn," he said. "I'm passing through.

Staying at your Slippery Eel. Came to take pictures of your islands."

He asked to be forgiven again. He took our silence for coldness, a desire to be left alone. He bowed, continued on his way.

"Please," said Mum.

He paused, looked back at us.

"We have few pictures of ourselves," she said. "Could we have the one you've taken today?"

He grinned, and we came back fully into the world, and Mum asked him into our sandy garden for tea.

He told us of his travels, of faraway cities and mountains and seas. He said he loved the feeling of moving through the world, light and free, moving through other people's stories. Sometimes, he said, when he got his photographs home, they were like images from dreams and legends. He laughed with delight at Stupor Bay. He swept his hands toward the sea and the islands.

"Who'd've guessed a place like this was waiting for me."

We said we'd hardly ever moved from this place, and for the first time, as I looked at Benn, I found myself thinking that one day we might move away.

He told us about America, and the kids called Maggie and Jason.

"You got the perfect gifts for them," he said.

He bought a rock painted with the face of a grinning angel and the seashell model of a mermaid.

He sipped his tea and ate his scone. He took more photographs of us and of the shack and the islands.

"I always take home tales as well," he said.

He winked at Mum.

"You look like you might know a tale or two."

That night Mum sang shanties in the Slippery Eel. I sat with Benn and drank lemonade and nibbled crisps. Between the songs he told me of all the seas he'd seen around the world. He dipped the tip of his finger into his beer.

"An atom of the water in this," he said, "was one day in the Sea of Japan." He dipped his finger again. "And an atom of this was in the Bay of Bengal. All seas flow into each other." He licked his finger, laughed. "And into us."

I swigged my lemonade. I felt the Baltic Sea and the Yellow Sea and the Persian Gulf pour through me. Rain pattered on the window at our backs. Mum's voice danced around the music of a flute. We joined in with the choruses. We tapped the rhythms on the table. Benn drank and told me of his home and his family so many miles away.

"I'm happy when I'm there," he said. "But then I travel, and I find so many places to be happy in."

Mum's singing ended and she sat between me and Benn, and her voice was edged with laughter. At closing time we stood outside. The rain had stopped, the clouds had dispersed, the moon was out. The sea thundered on the shore.

"I'll do those pics tonight," he said. "Use nighttime as a darkroom."

He touched Mum's face. He told her she was beautiful. I turned away. They whispered. I think they kissed.

The man with the fin surfaced in my dreams. I spoke the watery words for "dad." He spoke the airy words for "daughter." We swam together to southern seas of colored fish and coral, to northern seas of icebergs and whales. We swam all night from sea to sea to sea to sea, and when I woke, the sun was up and there were already voices in the garden.

"Come and see," said Mum when I appeared at the door.

Her eyes were wide and shining.

"Come and see," said Benn.

I walked barefoot through the sand. There were photographs scattered on the garden table. Mum held another photograph against her breast.

"You ever see one of these things develop?" said Benn.

I shook my head.

"At first the things in them are seen like secret things, through liquid—like secret creatures glimpsed beneath the sea. They're seen by a strange pale light that shines just like a moon." He narrowed his eyes, gazed at me, smiled. "These are the secrets I glimpsed last night, Annie Lumsden."

Then he stepped away from us, faced the islands, left us alone.

I sifted through the photos on the table: Mum and me, the garden, the shack, the islands. Mum still held the other to her breast.

"Look, Annie," she said.

She bit her lip as she tilted the photograph over at last and let me see.

There we were, Mum and me at the water's edge. Like Benn said, it was like I was something washed up by the sea, like Mum was reaching out to help me up, to help me to be born. I saw how seaweedy my hair truly was, how sealy my skin was. Then I looked away, looked back again, but it was true. A fin was growing at my back. Narrow, pale, half formed, like it was just half grown, but it was a fin.

Mum touched me there now, below my neck, between my shoulders. She traced the line of my spine. I touched where she touched, but we touched only me.

"Nothing there?" I whispered.

"Nothing there."

I traced the same line on the photograph. I looked at Benn, straight and tall, facing the islands and the sea.

"Could Benn . . . ?" I started.

"How could you think such a thing?" said Mum.

I looked at her.

"So the tale was true?" I said.

She smiled into my eyes.

"Aye. The tale was true."

And I pushed the photograph into her hand, and ran away from her and ran past Benn, and ran into the waves and didn't stop until I'd plunged down deep and burst back up again and swum and felt the joy of the fin quivering at my back, supporting me, helping me forward.

I looked back, saw Mum and Benn at the water's edge, hand in hand.

"You saw the truth!" I yelled.

"And the truth can set you free!" Benn answered back.

He went away soon afterward. He said he had a boxer to see in London and maybe an actress in Milan, and there was a war he needed to attend to in the Far East, and . . . He shrugged. Must seem a shapeless, aimless life to folk like us, he said.

"You get yourself to the States one day," he said to me. "You go and see my Maggie."

I gulped.

"I will," I said, and as I said it I believed it.

"Good. And you can be sure she'll know your tale by then."

We waited with him for a taxi outside the Slippery Eel. He had his painted rock and his shell mermaid. He held Mum tight and kissed her.

I held the shell that Mum had given me.

"Can I . . . ?" I said to her.

She smiled and nodded.

"It's for you," I said to Benn. "And then for Maggie."

He held it to his ear.

"I hear the roaring of the sea. I hear the whisper of its secrets. I hear the silence of its depths." He winked. "I know it's very precious, Annie. I'll keep it safe."

And he kissed me on the brow. Then the taxi came, and the man from America left Stupor Bay.

Afterward things were never quite the same. Things that'd seemed fixed and hard and hopeless started to shift. Words stopped being barnacles. Numbers were no longer limpets. I started to feel as free on land as I did in the sea. I fell less and less. Mrs. McLintock started talking about trying me in a school again. Was it to do with Mum's tales and Benn's photograph? One day I dared to tell Dr. John about the man with the fin. He laughed and laughed. I dared to show him Benn's picture and he laughed again. Then he went quiet.

"Sometimes," he said, "the best way to understand how to be human is to understand our strangeness."

He asked to look at my back. He peeped down beneath the back of my collar.

"Nothing there?" I said.

"Yes. There is an astonishing thing there. A mystery. And sometimes the biggest mystery of all is how a mystery might help to solve another mystery." Then he laughed again. "Pick the sense out of that!" he said.

He smiled.

"Come back in a year's time, Annie Lumsden," he said.

And, of course, it was all to do with simple growing up, with being thirteen, heading for fourteen and beyond. And it was to do with having a mum who thought there was nothing strange in loving a daughter who might be half a creature from the sea.

The library was a couple of streets away from home: a small branch library, the kind of place we all take for granted, the kind of place that wrong-headed people say has outlived its time. It was close to Felling Square and the Victoria Jubilee pub, where folk gathered around the piano in a side room to sing old songs and tell old tales. And it was just across the street from a patch of grass where I played football as a boy. On one side of the road, as I ran around with Peter, Kev, Colin, and Tex, I imagined being a famous footballer. On the other, I dreamed of being a published author. I'd often go into the library at dusk, when we couldn't see the ball any more. As my footballing dreams receded and my writerly dreams increased, I'd go in wearing Levi's and Ben Sherman instead of muddy jeans and battered football cleats. I remember reading John Wyndham, Irving Stone, Charles

Williams, Morris West. I thought I looked very modern and sophisticated when I took books from the Recommended New Novels section, though I often felt rather confused. I recall the exact moment I drew Hemingway's short-story collection, *The First Forty-Nine Stories*, from a shelf. I felt a shock of recognition as I opened it and began to read. I'd always known that I wanted to be a writer, and suddenly I had an idea of what kind of writer I wanted to be. This strange serendipitous mixture of discovery and recognition would be repeated in that building as I grew older — the first reading of D. H. Lawrence, for instance, or Stevie Smith.

For most of my teenage years I was fascinated by the paranormal. I loved the library's Religion and Philosophy section, skimming past the books about worthy saints and famous thinkers and seeking the barmier books, to plunder them for information about ghosts and spirits, clairvoyance, spontaneous combustion, levitation, spirit writing, human vanishings — and poltergeists. It was said that the most disturbing books about such matters, too dangerous to be allowed freely into the world, were locked away in a secret room over the hill in the central library in Gateshead. One I especially hungered for became legendary to me: *The Projection of the Astral Body* by Carrington and Muldoon. I never found it. I was also a fan of Hammer horror films, of TV's *The Twilight Zone* and of Dennis Wheatley's weird and terrifying novels, such as *The Devil Rides Out* and *The Ka of Gifford Hillary*. I loved *The Third Eye* by T. Lobsang Rampa. It told of Lobsang's boyhood in the monasteries and mountains of Tibet, his initiation into ancient mysteries, the operation on his skull that opened up his powers of clairvoyance. I dreamed of being him. I walked through the streets of Felling trying to feel possessed by him. Then it turned out that Lobsang was a hoaxer. He was Cyril Hoskin, a plumber's son from Devon, and he'd never stepped foot outside the British Isles. How disgraceful! But it didn't matter to me. Wasn't that what writers were supposed to do — make things up, make lies seem like truth, create new versions of themselves? I read a lot about Buddhism, chanted the Upanishads to myself, practiced yoga, stood on my head beside my bed, breathed *Om Om Om*, tried to meditate. I spent night after night attempting to travel in the astral plane, just like Lobsang did. No success. If only I'd been able to get my hands on that book by Carrington and Muldoon . . .

The world was striving to be new. All across Tyneside, the old dark terraced streets were being torn down. Estates in bright new brick and pebble-dash, like Leam Lane Estate in this story, were spreading out across the open spaces. New tower blocks rose all over the landscape. Politicians talked about a world of white-hot technology; we were about to send a man to the moon; *Tomorrow's World* on the BBC told us about cures for cancer, driverless cars, paper pants, self-cleaning clothes, giant carrots, robots, laser beams, jet packs. What a future was to come!

But the past, and ancient superstitions and religious beliefs, kept reasserting themselves. St. Patrick's Church was packed with people of all ages. I was an altar boy until I was about fifteen, serving at Masses and weddings and funerals. Like most of my friends, I continued to take Communion and go to confession. Every year a planeful of St. Patrick's parishioners flew to Lourdes in France with the priest to see the miracles and healings, and to pray to Our Lady to be healed themselves. Many of my relatives — my grandma, my Uncle Maurice, my Auntie Anne — went on these trips. They came home, their eyes shining, carrying Our Lady–shaped bottles of holy water that we used along with medicines to treat coughs and colds, and much more serious diseases. And there were plaster statues and prayer cards, and garish plastic grottos with lights that flashed around Our Lady and the kneeling St. Bernadette.

Tales and rumors showed how difficult it was for some folk to adjust to the new world. They kept ponies in their brand-new dining rooms and chickens on their balconies. Old women read each other's tea leaves in Dragone's. There were tales of weeping statues. Superstitions abounded: don't walk under ladders, don't cross on the stairs, never open an umbrella indoors, don't spill salt, always leave a house through the same door by which you entered . . . There were tales of ghosts and hauntings in the brightly lit brick and pebble-dashed homes. As in the story of Joe Quinn and his poltergeist, a film crew did try to record the ghosts that walked at night and terrified a family in a brand-new house on Leam Lane Estate.

And, of course, despite the hopes inspired by some of the speakers on *Tomorrow's World*, death and sickness didn't go away. Despite modern medicine and surgery, Lourdes water and prayer, I lost my dad to cancer when I was fifteen. And just like Davie, the narrator of the story, I lost a sister, too. Barbara was only a year old when she died; I was seven.

joe quinn's poltergeist

So, I'm in Holly Hill Park with Geordie Craggs. We're watching the lasses play tennis when Joe Quinn saunters through the gate.

"Pretend we've not seen," I say.

No good. He heads straight for us. He's got a packet of coconut mushrooms and he's holding them out.

Stupid Geordie takes one. He even says ta.

"Have another," says Joe. "Gan on. I've got tons."

Maria Caldwell jumps high and grunts, and smashes the ball straight into the fence.

"Prefer a Midget Gem?" says Joe to me. "I've got some of them and all."

"No," I mutter.

"Nowt wrong with being friendly," he says.

"I'll have one," says Geordie, and Joe smiles and sits down on the grass close by.

It's the middle of the afternoon, the middle of the holidays, and hot as Hell. The air's shimmering and you can feel the heat rising from the earth. Josephine Minto wipes her forehead with a towel, swigs from a bottle of lemonade, or something, and gets ready to serve. She looks over to check I'm still watching. She's the best—it's obvious. She'll win easily. The yellow ball's a blur as it flashes over the net. Maria doesn't even see it. I want to cheer, but I don't.

"I've got a poltergeist," says Joe as Josephine gets ready to serve again.

"A what?" says Geordie.

"Poltergeist."

I spit. Typical Joe bliddy Quinn.

"What's one of them?" asks Geordie.

"Kind of ghost," says Joe. "Davie'll know. Davie?"

I say nothing.

"There was stuff flying all over the house the other

night," Joe goes on. "Cups and plates and stuff."

"Stuff flying?" says Geordie.

"That's what they do, poltergeists. They send everything barmy."

Geordie's mouth dropped open.

"There's a window smashed and all, and a door's hangin' off its hinges."

"Hell's teeth."

"Aye," says Joe. "Me mam says it's a sign of disturbance in the spirit world. Or the house has entered some kind of vortex or something."

"Vortex," says Geordie.

"Geordie, man," I mutter.

"I knaa," says Joe. "Hard to believe, eh? Mebbe you should come and see for yoursels?"

"Could we?" says Geordie.

"That is, if you're not too scared."

"'Course we're not, are we, Davie? When should we come?"

"It starts happenin' round about teatime. So come for tea. Come today. I'll tell me mam to put some extra chips on, eh?"

Geordie's all wide-eyed.

"Aye," he says. "Alreet, Joe."

Joe gets up and walks away.

"Flying cups!" says Geordie.

I sigh. Stupid Geordie. Joe turns round and lobs a few Midget Gems at us. Geordie catches none of them and starts picking them out of the grass. Josephine squeals and yells, "Game and first set to Miss Minto!"

"Broken windows!" Geordie gasps. "Do you think we'll really see it?"

"Aye," I say. "We'll see it's just daft Joe Quinn and his even dafter mother."

"Worth having a look though, eh? You've said yourself that the world's a weird place."

"But I didn't mean Joe Quinn, and I didn't mean bliddy poltergeists."

He jams a few gems into his mouth.

"At least we'll get some chips."

Joe Quinn. What a dreamer. Take his dad, for instance. If he wasn't a hit man in Arizona, he was robbing banks in China; he'd stashed away a million quid in Chile for Joe's future; he'd send flight tickets for Joe when he was eighteen and they'd live the lives of outlaws. Turned out he was in Durham Prison for beating a bloke half to death on Newcastle Quayside one Friday night.

"Aye," said Joe when we found out. "But it took half a dozen coppers to bring him in, and he only done it because the bloke impugned me mother."

"Impugned?" I said.

"That's the word. And there's no way me dad could let that happen to me mam."

The mother. She was another one. She'd been on tours with the Rolling Stones; she'd danced for the King of Thailand; she'd dined with Nikita Khrushchev.

"So what you doing on Leam Lane Estate?" I said.

"It's just till I get some education under me belt. And till me dad gets out. Then she says the world's our oyster."

Joe Quinn. He was the one who laughed when my sister died. He was the one who asked what the blubbing was for. I don't think he even remembers. It was years ago. To him it was just nowt. And now it's poltergeists. Hell's teeth.

Anyway, we go. We wait till Josephine's got game, set, and match. She looks at me and I look at her, and we both hesitate, and I wonder, should I tell Geordie to go to Joe's himself? But I don't, and we head off. No need to tell our mams. Mine'll think I'm at Geordie's, his'll think he's at mine. We pass the new priest, Father Kelly, as we leave the park. He's standing under a cherry tree, in his long black robe, smoking. He waves at us. We wave back.

We walk down The Drive. We're parched, so we stop at Wiffen's and buy some pop.

"We're bliddy daft," I say. "It's a wild goose chase."

"Flying plates, man!" says Geordie. "Smashed windows!"

He starts on about the ghost they had at Wilfie Mack's house a couple of years back, the one where the telly reporter and the cameraman stayed all night to watch for it.

"And they saw absolutely nowt," I say.

"Aye, but they said they definitely felt something. And there was that weird shadow. Remember, Davie?"

I shrug.

"And look what happened to Wilfie just two weeks later."

"Aye," I say finally, and shudder, despite the baking heat.

We reach the estate and turn into Sullivan Street. Lots of the front doors are wide open. Some of them have got stripy plastic curtains dangling, to keep the flies out. A gang of half-naked kids are playing football farther down the street. Their ball comes bouncing at us and they scream at us to kick it back. I do, and back it flies in a dead straight line.

No sign of anybody at Joe's. The curtains are closed at the front and the door's shut. We head down the side of the house. The back garden's baked mud and clay, hard as stone. It's dead quiet. Then suddenly the back door's wide open and Joe's there, grinning. Mrs. Quinn's behind him with her arms crossed.

"Hello, boys," she says. "Why don't you step inside?"

The kitchen table's set. There's fruit punch, tomato sauce, and a big pile of bread and butter.

"Joe said you'd like some chips," she says.

She slides cut potatoes into boiling fat.

"Sit down," she says. "Could be a while."

"That's right," says Joe. "Doesn't just come to order."

She laughs, and tousles his hair.

"Do your mams know you're here?" she says.

"No," we tell her.

She shakes the chips.

"You're the one whose sister died, aren't you?" she says to me.

I flinch.

"Aye," I say.

"Any sign of her since?"

"What?"

She smiles.

"Never mind," she says. "Look. That's the broken window Joe told you about."

It's the narrow pane at the top of the kitchen window. I imagine a knife flying through it, or a fork.

"I should put Sellotape or something over it," she says. "But it's nice to have a bit of breeze in this heat. Joe, show them the plates, son."

He opens the drawer in the table, and takes out some broken bits of cups and plates, and puts them in front of us.

"Ever seen owt like that?" he asks. He holds up a jagged bit in wonder.

"They were ordinary proper plates," he says, "and then . . ."

There's a record player on the kitchen bench. His mam drops a record onto the turntable. A voice and a guitar start wailing.

"You won't have heard this," she tells us. "They're underground, from California."

She starts dancing, swinging her arms around her head and her hair falls back and forward over her shoulders. She's got her eyes closed, as if she's in a dream. I can't help watching. She's not like any other mams I know. A slice of bread and butter flies over her head and slaps onto the kitchen wall. Geordie gasps and curses and looks at me, but nobody else says anything. It's like Joe and his mother haven't seen.

Soon the chips are done.

Mrs. Quinn tips them into a bowl, leans over the table, and puts them onto our plates.

"Tuck in," she says.

I make a butty, a layer of chips and tomato sauce between two slices of bread. Lovely. Then another slice of bread and butter flies across the room.

Geordie bursts out laughing.

"That was you!" he says to Joe.

Joe just shakes his head and goes on eating. His mam leans over us. Her hair is yellow as corn. I can feel her breath on me.

"Maybe you have to believe that," she says to Geordie. "But, Davie, I think you're different. What did you see? How do you explain it?"

There's no way to answer. I take another bite of my

171

butty. Geordie's sniggering at my side. Mrs. Quinn rests her hand on my head.

"Just be quiet for a moment," she says to me. "Relax and try to feel what is happening in this place. Feel what Joe and I feel, even on a sunny afternoon in an ordinary house on an ordinary estate. There is a disturbance. We are passing through some kind of vortex. Can you feel it, Davie?"

I can feel that Geordie wants to get away but I can't move.

Mrs. Quinn moves her hand over my scalp and I go dizzy.

"Just imagine," she murmurs, "what it is like at night, when the chairs are shifting and the doors are banging and . . ."

Geordie snorts.

There's a dog howling somewhere. There's the sound of something breaking upstairs.

Mrs. Quinn takes her hand away. She stares at the ceiling.

"Did you sense something?" she says softly.

I don't know how to answer.

"You did," she says. "I know it. Only special people can. We are surrounded by strange forces."

Geordie snorts again. He stuffs some chips into his mouth.

"Howay, Davie," he says. "Time to go."

"You're a churchgoer, aren't you, Davie?" says Mrs. Quinn. "Yes, I know you are. You understand things like this, don't you? Things beyond our ken."

"Ken who?" mutters Geordie.

"And you have your priests," Mrs. Quinn goes on. "Maybe you could talk of this to your priest. Maybe he could come and rid us of our poltergeist and bring this house some peace. Maybe he'll feel it's his duty."

I get up. A few chips bounce off the opposite wall.

She holds my arm a moment. She breathes into my ear.

"You'll ask him, will you, Davie? Just for me?"

I try to imagine telling all this to Father O'Mahoney. I see him rolling his eyes at such nonsense, telling me to go for a good long run or to say ten Hail Marys and a Glory Be.

"Aye," I mutter.

We head for the door.

"Duck!" yells Joe.

A plate or something crashes into the wall.

"It's getting worse!" he cries.

"Begone!" shouts Mrs. Quinn. "Begone, ye demon poltergeist!"

I run with Geordie past the footballing kids. He's laughing his head off. I'm trembling in fright.

I dream that night, of course I do. There's flying chips and bread and butter and knives and forks, and Geordie's howling like a dog. Josephine's hitting a tennis ball again and again over my head. Mam wakes me in the morning and I jump as if she's a ghost come up from Hell to get me.

I ask her straight away, like it's part of the dream, "Did she ever come back, Mam?"

"What on earth's the matter with you?" she says. She strokes my head gently. "And did who ever come back?"

"Barbara," I say.

"Barbara?"

"Yes."

"Oh, son. What kind of dream were you having?"

"She couldn't . . . could she?"

"No."

"Could she?"

Mam goes still.

"There was just the one time. . . ."

She looks away. She touches her cheek with her fingertip the way she does.

"What time?" I whisper.

"I felt her touch me, son, on my shoulder. A couple of weeks after . . ."

I wait. I watch.

"I heard her whispering, 'I'm all right, Mammy. Don't worry, Mammy, I'm all right.'"

"Did you see her?"

"No. And it was just the once. Maybe it was just a . . . But it felt like her, son. It made me feel . . . I didn't feel so desolate." She sighs. "I didn't tell you. I didn't want to upset you."

Then her eyes are shining as she smiles.

"Look at that sun," she says. "What a summer we're having, eh?"

"Aye."

"You'll be seeing Geordie, eh?"

"Aye."

She smiles again.

"She'll always love us, won't she?" she says. "And we'll always love her."

She leans down to kiss my cheek.

"Come on, then," she says. "Up and out and off you go. Have fun."

"Did you believe it, mam?"

"That she came back for a moment? I felt her and heard her so I suppose I have to. Come on. Up and out. The day's already flying by."

I head for Geordie's but I keep scanning the streets for Josephine. I pass by the park and listen for the pop and thump of racquets and balls. When I turn the corner by the Co-op, I bump right into Father Kelly in his long black gown. He's the new young priest, straight from Ireland. He's leaning against the wall of the shop like he's been bliddy lying in wait for me. He laughs and takes a deep drag of his cigarette.

"Having a quick fag, Davie," he says. "Getting up me strength to pay a visit to Mrs. Malone."

"Oh," I say.

"She'd test the faith of St. bliddy Francis himself," he says. He makes a quick sign of the cross. "'Scuse the French. Off to Geordie's, are you?"

"Yes, Father."

"Good lad. Make the most of it." He holds out his cigarette. "Want a drag or two?"

I don't move. He laughs again.

"I know some of you boys get started early."

He smokes then flicks the cigarette away. I want to move on but I can't. It seems like he's the same.

"You know her?" he says. "The Missus Malone?"

"A bit, Father."

"They say she's lapsed," he tells me. "They say other things."

He lights another cigarette.

"You've heard?" he asks.

"Dunno, Father."

"Best not to. These things are sent to test us."

He shields his eyes from the sun's glare and looks around. I still can't move.

"Father," I say.

"Yes?"

"I think I'm starting to believe in things I shouldn't."

"Protestantism?" he says.

"No, Father."

"Atheism?"

"No, Father."

I hear kids laughing in the park.

"It's never Sunderland!" he exclaims.

"No, Father."

"Well, that all seems pretty safe. Your seat in Heaven is assured."

He moves his hand through the air in blessing.

"Things like ghosts," I blurt out. "Things like that."

"Jesus, ye'd be at home in Ireland, lad."

"Poltergeists."

"They're the best, eh? Flinging stuff here, there, and everywhere."

"So they're real?"

"Real? What's real? The air's real. Can you see it? God's real. Can you see him? And the Devil. Or mebbe God and the Devil is all of this. You and me and that tree over there, and those birds above and the wall of the bliddy Co-op." He sighs. "That's heresy, though. Forget I said it."

I catch the scent of wine or something on his breath. Maybe altar wine from this morning's Mass.

"Poltergeists," he says. "Now I'd like to see one of those boys in action."

"Would you?" I say.

"Who wouldn't?"

He takes a deep drag on his cigarette, then drops it suddenly, stamps it out, and heads off to Mrs. Malone's.

★　　★　　★

Geordie wants to play football and we kick around for a bit in his front street, but I'm hopeless. I can't help it. I'm drawn back to Joe's. Can't think about anything else. I tell him I think we should go again.

"Did you not see?" Geordie says. "It was Joe chucking all the stuff around. It's just Joe bliddy Quinn being Joe bliddy Quinn. And she's letting him."

"There was something," I say.

"So now you're sticking up for him when you're the one who always says he's just a freak."

"I'm not sticking up for him! It's nothing to do with him. It's—"

He snorts.

"Oh, I impugn you!" he mocks. "I am so sorry. We are surrounded by strange forces!"

He chips the ball into the air, knees it, heads it, then lashes it into the front garden wall.

He leaps high and punches the air.

"Goaaaaal!" he yells. "Right into the top corner of the vortex!"

Then he turns to me.

"You won't catch me in that damn loony bin again," he says.

I turn away.

"Begone!" he yells, and he screeches like a demon.

I go up onto the top fields and lie there, and the long grass waves above my eyes. The sun's bright, the sky's blue, the larks are singing wild. Sometimes a thin cloud drifts by. I sit up and look down at everything: the town, its square, its streets, its new estates, its steeples and parks. Hear the drone of traffic and engines. The dinning of caulkers in the shipyards on the river far below. Kids squealing somewhere. I'm sure I can hear the pop of tennis balls. I see a lad and his lass walk through the grass a hundred yards away then lie down in it together.

The heat comes from the earth and from the sky. The distant sea's dark blue. Is this everything, all this stuff around me? Is this where everything happens? I think of Barbara, the way she used to giggle and wave as I arrived home from school. I think of Josephine Minto, her eyes, her hair, the way her legs move as she leaps, the way Barbara would have turned out if she'd not died. I think of Joe Quinn's poltergeist. I think of God. I watch the shadows getting longer down in the pale streets of Leam Lane. Somebody cries in joy or pain, and after an age I get up and move on. My body moves but I feel like I'm not part of it. What am I? Body, brain, soul, or all of these? Infant, boy, man, or all those things together? Or nothing, just nothing at all?

"Davie!" yells somebody, some kid playing with other kids on the playing fields. I wave but don't know who it is.

"Davie!" he yells again, and keeps on yelling as I walk on, "Davie, Davie Davie!" till the word means nowt; is just a sound, just part of all the sounds around me and inside me. *Davie, Davie, Davie . . .*

Time's flying and it's already darkening as I enter Sullivan Street again. I don't go to the house. I play football with the half-naked skinny kids till we can hardly see the ball and the lights in the houses are being switched on. It must be late. Mothers start calling and one by one the kids begin to disappear. I smell food cooking. There're songs and laughter. I watch Joe's house. Did a curtain move? Did I hear something breaking? Then the screaming starts. High-pitched, incomprehensible. It must be Mrs. Quinn. I realize there's someone at my shoulder, a woman, and other women and men gathering in the gloom, and knots of kids. Then there's the sound of breaking glass.

"It's a bliddy madhouse," someone mutters.

"And wait till the bliddy bloke gets out," another says.

A little girl starts crying.

Then Joe's outside with us, hurrying from the house. There's a dark patch on his brow that must be blood. He comes straight to me.

"Davie!" he gasps. "Come and see!"

I step back.

"Come on!" he says. "It's like it's getting wilder just for you!"

"What do you mean, for me?"

"I knew you must be here. It's like you bring more energy or something. It's like—"

Behind him there's a crash, another splintering of glass. He tugs my arm. I break free, turn, and run from Sullivan Street. I hear him calling my name and laughing as I go. Thrown stones skitter and skip around my feet.

I meet Father Kelly in the street again, two days later. This time he's stepping out of the Columba Club, and this time there's beer on his breath. He's still in his black robes in this August heat. A wooden crucifix dangles from his throat.

He laughs.

"We meet again," he says. "Mebbe the good Lord has a plan for us."

He lights a cigarette.

"Missus Malone and I had a grand little meet," he says.

"That's good, Father."

"Aye. She's a one, eh? And how's all that believing stuff you were on about?"

"The same, Father."

"Don't think too much. That's probably the answer." He winks. "Or have a pint or two."

"I've got a poltergeist, Father," I say.

"Have you now?"

"Yes, Father."

"There's a thing. And where might you be keeping this poltergeist?"

"In Sullivan Street, Father."

He smiles. He pats my shoulder.

"Such lives you lads lead," he says.

"Will you come and see it, Father?"

"Let's see. I have to get the host to Mollie Carr.

There's Maurice Gadd that's had the stroke. Catechism catch-up for a husband that's decided to convert. And those wild McCracken bairns! They need to know the truth about the fires of Hell. . . . But I'm sure I can fit in a poltergeist or three."

"It usually starts late afternoon."

He tousles my hair.

"Late afternoon. Sullivan Street. I'll see you there."

He winks and taps his nose.

"And we'll not be mentioning this to Father O'Mahoney, will we, Davie?"

"No, Father."

"No indeed."

I join in with a great football match on the high field. There's dozens of us, from little kids to teenagers, rushing back and forward on the green. Must be twenty, twenty-five a side. We run, we yell, do long sliding tackles, leap high to try to head the flying ball. I take a shot that swerves just past the post. Another wallops into Billy Campbell's belly. I have a little run, beat one man, then two, rush on, tumble, jump up again. I lose myself. I'm not me—I'm a proper player. I'm at Wembley, at St. James's Park, and all the others are too. We struggle for our teams. One side leads and then the other, then the first fights back again. In dashing through the field and playing with the ball we change ourselves, we change the world. Our muscles ache, our hearts thump, our lungs are fit to burst. We laugh and groan and cheer and yell.

"YEEESS! YEEEESSSSSS! OH YES!"

And afterward I walk with Geordie through the light. In the sky above the sea there's something sparkling. The larks sing high over our heads. A butterfly lands on Geordie's collar. I gently touch it free and we watch it fly away. He tells me that he heard Josephine asking about me, and that he sees why I say she's beautiful. I tell him I'm trying to sort out the poltergeist.

"Sort it out?"

"What it is. Why it's there."

"It's him. It's her. That's all."

"Father Kelly is going to look."

"To look and then to say it's all a load of crap."

"We'll see."

I hurry home and grab some bread and cheese, and hurry out again.

"No time to stop?" says Mam.

I shake my head.

"Places to go," she sighs. "People to see. A life to live."

I hesitate a second, catch her eye.

"OK?" she whispers.

"Aye. OK."

"We quiver on the edge of an immensity," says Father Kelly. We've encountered each other on the road down to Leam Lane. "It is outside us and within. I knew it as a boy, looking at the sky, looking at the starsh, looking at myshelf." His voice is slipping. "I knew it looking out upon the ocean from the hillsh of Kerry." He lights a cigarette. "Don't get into theshe," he says. He takes a little silver flask from his robe and sips from it. "Don't get into drink," he says. His hand is shaking as he points across the earth, the sea, the sky. "I shee it here as you do. I know you shee how it all quakes and shines and trembles, Davie. I know you hear how it hums and shings."

We walk on. We come to Sullivan Street.

"And don't get into God," he whispers, as if he's speaking to himself. "Don't get into none of that."

★　　★　　★

We are unexpected, of course. Mrs. Quinn is lying on a battered sun lounger in the back garden with her skirt pulled up to her thighs. Underground music drifts from the house. Joe is nowhere to be seen.

"I brought a priest," I say unnecessarily.

"Did you now?" says Mrs. Quinn.

She regards the man at my side, his long black gown, black sandals, crucifix, bare white calves.

"My name ish Father Kelly," he says.

"Rosemary Quinn," she says.

"Davie told me of your dishturbance."

"Did he now? Can I get you a cup of tea? Or there may be a bottle or two of beer around." She stands up. She tugs the straps of her sundress back up onto her shoulders. "So have you come to calm it?"

He shrugs.

"It was not part of my training, Mrs. Quinn, but there ish maybe something that I . . ."

"Joe!" calls Mrs. Quinn. "Joe! Davie's here with the priest to see the poltergeist!"

A cup flies down from an open upstairs window and bounces in the grass.

"OK!" yells Joe. "I'm coming down."

Inside the kitchen, fragments of broken crockery lie

against the skirting boards. There's a new little jagged hole in one of the windows. Strips of wallpaper are curling from the walls. Joe comes downstairs with an orange Elastoplast on his brow.

"And look at this," he says.

He lifts up a chair and shows that one of its legs has been ripped off.

"Just came down one morning and there it was like this," he says.

His mother stares at the priest.

"What is doing this?" she says. "What are these strange forces?"

She holds out a bottle of beer and a glass to him. He pours carefully. He drinks. She stands close, leans up to him.

"Is it God?" she whispers. She widens her eyes. "Or is it that Devil, Father?"

A knife clatters against the wall. The priest flinches. He looks at Joe, at me. He drinks. There's a sound of something shattering upstairs.

We all stand silent, we listen and watch. A dog howls. The sun is sinking over the estate. I am poised to be terrified, to be illuminated, for the forces to work again. For a while nothing more happens. There's just stillness, silence and the immensity within and outside us. We all sigh.

"You must be hungry, Father," says Mrs. Quinn. "I'll put some chips on, shall I?"

"Aye," he says, "I have had a day without much nourishment in it."

"And you lads," she says. "Why don't you go outside, enjoy the last rays of the sun. And give that poor mutt a drink."

We do. We perch on the edge of the sun lounger.

"Is it you?" I say.

"'Course it's not. In fact, according to me dad, it's him."

"What?"

"We went to see him in jail on Sunday. What a bliddy nightmare place. He said he'd been focusing his thoughts on the house, making things move by the power of his will."

"What? Why?"

Joe holds out a packet of cigarettes to me. I don't take one. He lights one for himself and blows the smoke across my face.

"I think he's mebbe trying to harm us," he says. "He's coming up with all these tales of what me mother's doing while he's inside. I think he's goin' bliddy mad, Davie. You should see how wild his eyes are now. You should see how scared the officers are of him. He's turnin' to a bliddy monster! How's Josephine?"

"Eh?"

"You shagged her yet?"

A clod of earth flies up from the ground and over our heads.

"That was you!" I cry.

"No, it wasn't. Have you, eh?"

I'm about to go for him but his mother's at the door. The chips are done. We go inside and sit at the little Formica table. Father Kelly's into the second bottle of beer. The air is golden through the broken window. The chips, the sauce, and the bread are all delicious. My mug of tea trembles as I lift it. It tilts and tea splashes down onto the table top. Mrs. Quinn puts her hand over mine.

"You OK, Davie?" she says.

"Aye."

Father Kelly smiles.

"The boy—like all boys—ish prey to great forces, great hungers, great emotionsh."

He chews his chips. He swigs his beer. He doesn't

flinch as a plate spins from the table to the floor. He leans forward and speaks in hushed tones, as if to communicate with nobody but himself.

"In Ireland," he says, "such things were known, before the dead hand of the Church took us in its dreadful grip."

He laughs. He stands up and flings his plate with its last few chips against the kitchen wall.

"Forgive me, Mrs. Quinn," he says. "I will pay for the damage, of course."

"Oh, no need, Father."

He laughs again, loudly. He picks up his glass and flings that against the wall too.

"Another beer, perhaps?" says Mrs. Quinn. "You boys . . ."

Joe takes my arm and leads me out. He shuts the door. We start fighting straight away. We punch each other, grab each other's throats, shove each other's heads onto the ground. We struggle and kick and roll and grunt. At last I get him properly down and I straddle him. Blood from my nose drips down onto him.

"I'll effing kill you, Quinn," I say.

"Why's that, then?" he snarls.

"Because you don't know bliddy why, that's why!"

"What a load of bliddy crap! Go on, then. Do it! Ha!" His face twists into a sneer. "You haven't got the bliddy guts."

I spit on him. He spits upward at me. Saliva and snot and blood dangle and drop in the air between us. We struggle on, but in the end it all disgusts me and I roll away, groaning and cursing at the sky.

Joe gets up onto the sun lounger. He lights a cigarette.

A full moon's already shining in the sky. There are moths already flying. Bats already flicker in the white late light. We say nowt for ages.

"It drives you mad," I say at last.

"What does?" answers Joe.

"The bliddy moon."

"Bliddy thing!" He shakes his fist at it. "Bliddy stupid round thing shining in the sky!"

I watch it shining down on him.

"You ever want to kill everything?" he says.

"Aye."

"Really?"

"Aye. Every bliddy thing that lives and that has ever lived."

"And God?"

"Aye, him. Pummel him to bliddy dust."

"Aye! Ha! Aye!"

I look at him through the moonlight. His eyes are glittering like mine must be. His face is shining. His heart is bursting like mine, and his mind is yearning and his soul is soaring. We know we're just the same. And in the weird mix of silver light and dark between us, things begin to rise. Just little things—broken stems of weeds, tiny twigs, fallen flowers, scraps of paper, fragments of dust and bits of stone. They rise and hang there, shining where the moonlight touches them, as if it is the light that holds them suspended. They shift and slowly spin as the air moves past them. It only lasts a few short seconds then they fall again and there's only emptiness where they once were, and the possibility that things like them might rise again.

Joe breathes smoke into the moonlight.

"Was that you?" he says.

But there's no way to answer, we both know that.

The darkness darkens and the moonlight brightens. I know it's time to move but I don't, not until the priest comes out again.

"Still here, Davie?" he asks.

"Aye, Father."

"So let's go off together, eh?"

"Aye, Father."

He laughs.

"You have a splendid poltergeist, Joe Quinn," he says.

Joe laughs too. Upstairs, beyond the open window, something breaks.

"Thanks, Father," says Joe.

Inside, Mrs. Quinn is singing.

I walk with the priest out of Leam Lane. We take the road between the dark fields and the town. We hear laughter, sudden cries, the hooting of an owl, the beating of the engines at the heart of everything.

"There is no God," says Father Kelly.

"I know that, Father."

"There is no Heaven to go to. And no Hell."

"I know that, Father."

"There's only us, and this."

"I know that, Father."

"But what an usness, and a thisness." He laughs at himself. "I couldn't have said such words an hour or two ago."

We separate at The Drive and go our different ways. I walk beneath dense trees. Nervous birds flutter in the nests above my head. I feel the thinness of me, the littleness of me, and the vastness and the weirdness of me. I become the darkness all around, I become the night. Tomorrow I will be a different Davie, and I will be the day. Suddenly I know the poltergeist is me. It is in me. It is me in fury at Joe Quinn, me in love with Josephine, me in hatred of the non-existent God; it is me in dread and bliddy grief, it is me in wonder at this place, this earth, this moon, this night. I know the poltergeist is all of us, raging and wanting to scream and to fight and to start flinging stuff; to smash and to break. It is all of us wanting to be still, to be quiet, to be in love, to be at peace.

I walk onward, begin to disappear, to truly be the dark.

And as I move through the black shadows cast by the dense overhanging shrubs of Sycamore Grove, I know that this should be the moment when I feel the gentle touch on my shoulder, and hear the longed-for whisper in my ear.

Of course they do not come.

Her touch will only come in dreams.

The whisper will be heard in stories that I'll come to tell.

She will be given endless life in memories and in words.

I walk on below the streetlights toward the square, toward my home.

Tomorrow I'll play football with Geordie and the lads on the high fields.

Soon I will kiss Josephine Minto beneath the cherry tree in Holly Hill Park.

Father Kelly will return to Ireland, where he will be unfrocked.

Mr. Quinn will kill a cellmate and will stay in jail.

Joe Quinn's poltergeist will disappear.

And there will be other occurrences, an immensity of them, and the world and all that's in it will continue to hum and sing, to shake and shine, to hold us in its darkness and its light.

By the time I was nineteen, I was at university. I'd grown my hair, I wore jeans and cheesecloth shirts, I listened to Pink Floyd and Leonard Cohen, and read Ginsberg and Dostoyevsky. I lived on a student grant — a very generous one, because my mother was a widow raising the family on her own. At the end of my first year I got a summer job in Swan Hunter's shipyard on the Tyne, and used the money from that to hitchhike away for a month in Greece with my girlfriend, Rhona. We met hundreds of others like ourselves: young, free, educated Western Europeans who roamed across the continent, who believed in love and peace. We slept on beaches, drank retsina, ate souvlaki, lay in the sun, swam in the warm Mediterranean sea.

When my dad had been nineteen, in 1942, the Second World War had already been going for three years. Both his education and his working life stopped. He was enlisted into the signals corp, taken away from the streets of Tyneside for military training in Glasgow. Then he was sent to the jungles of Burma to fight the Japanese. He wouldn't get home again until 1946. He married in 1948, and then we children began to come into the world.

He didn't talk much about his experiences of war and I don't remember asking him much about it. Maybe he encouraged me to think that as the days of war were gone, and it had all happened in a different age, I should keep on looking forward, moving forward. He believed in education, in progress. Like most men of his generation my father wanted his children to create a new and better world.

When I was growing up, the evidence of war was all around. There were ration books in Grandma's cupboard, and stifling gas masks that we used to wear to pretend we were monsters. I had a pair of trousers made from the blackout curtains that had once hung at my grandmother's window as the German bombers droned overhead. There was an abandoned gun emplacement beyond the playing fields, where mighty cannon had pointed toward the North Sea. On beautiful Northumbrian beaches, rows of huge concrete cubes stood below the dunes, designed to impede invasion from the sea. They're still there, all these years later, sinking inch by inch into the earth. So are the little pillboxes with horizontal slits for machine gunners. We used all these sites for our childhood games, and they infected our play. We played "Die the Best," shrieking with pain, flinging ourselves across the dunes, tottering in death agonies as the invaders came in. In the gardens, streets, and fields we played "Bomb Berlin," Germans versus English, English versus Japanese. We yelled out, *Achtung! Schnell! Banzai!* and *Die, you rat!* and ran with our arms spread wide like spitfire's wings, calling out, *Ratatatatat!*

In the adult world, deadlier games were played. Nuclear arsenals multiplied. Bombs were tested. Nervous and paranoid fingers hovered close to the button that could bring destruction to us all. The Iron Curtain was up. Bombs were raining down on Vietnam. Many thought that war had not really ended: that the peace in which we grew up was just a breathing space; that the worst was yet to come.

This is a story about the postwar world. The traumas of Eastern Europe are brought to Felling in the person of an East German boy, Klaus Vogel. The heroes of the story are the outsiders, Klaus Vogel and Mr. Eustace. I never knew any East German kids, but there were quite a number of Poles growing up among us — their families had escaped the invading Nazis just before the war. It was only later that I began to understand the deadly perils these families had lived through.

I knew about conchies — conscientious objectors — and how they were treated with contempt. Sometimes my friends and I wondered, What if war came back again? Would we join up? Would we fight, or would we be conchies? Would we be different from our fathers?

My dad died when I was fifteen and he was just forty-three. As a nineteen-year-old hitchhiking across Europe, I started to understand what he and men like him had gone through, what the whole world had gone through. I started to understand how privileged I was to grow up in a world without war, to be able to go to university, to grow my hair, to swim in the Med.

I set this story in the autumn, in what always seemed to be one of the darkest parts of Felling, beyond Watermill Lane, not too far from the graveyard at Heworth. There, trees hung heavy and dark over the pavements and verges. We often walked under them to play football on the broad playing field by Swards Road. It was best at dusk, as the stars came out above and frost began to glitter on the grass.

Klaus Vogel & the bad lads

We'd been together for years. We called ourselves the Bad Lads, but it was just a joke. We were mischief-makers, pests, and scamps. We never caused proper trouble—not till that autumn, anyway; round about the time we were turning thirteen; round about the time Klaus Vogel came.

The regulars were me, Tonto McKenna from Stivvey Court, Dan Digby, and the Spark twins, Fred and Frank. We all came from Felling and we all went to St. John's. Then there was Joe Gillespie. He was a year or so older than the rest of us, and kept himself a bit aloof, but he was the leader, and he was great. His hair was long and curled over his collar. He wore faded Levi's, Chelsea boots, Ben Sherman shirts. He had a girlfriend, Teresa Doyle. He used to walk hand in hand with her through Holly Hill Park. I used to dream about being just like Joe—flicking my hair back with my hand, winking at girls, putting my arm round one of the lads after a specially good stunt, saying, "We done really good, didn't we? We're really bad, aren't we? Ha ha ha!"

All of us, not just me, wanted to be a bit like Joe in those days.

Most days, after school, we took a ball onto the playing field at Swards Road and put two jumpers down for a goal. We played keep-up and penalties, practiced diving headers, swerves, and traps. We played matches with tiny teams and a single goal, but we still got carried away by it all, just like when we were eight or nine. We called each other Bestie, Pelé, Yashin, and commentated on the moves: "He's beaten one man; he's beaten two! Can he do it? *Yeees!* Oh no! Oh, what a save by the black-clad Russian!" We punched the air when we scored a goal and waved at the invisible roaring crowd. Our voices echoed across the playing field and over the rooftops. Our breath rose in plumes as the air chilled and the evening came on.

We felt ecstatic, transfigured. Then after a while one of us would see Joe coming out from among the houses, and we'd come back down to the real world.

Joe usually had a trick or two of his own lined up, but he always made a point of asking what we fancied doing next.

Tonto might say, "We could play knocky nine door in Balaclava Street."

Or Frank might go, "Jump through the hedges in Coldwell Park Drive?"

But we'd all just groan at things like that. They were little kids' tricks, and we'd done them tons of times before. Sometimes there were new ideas, like the night we howled like ghosts through Mrs. Minto's letter box, or when we phoned the police and said an escaped lunatic was chopping up Miss O'Sullivan in her front garden, or when we tied a length of string at head height right across Dunelm Terrace. But usually the best plans turned out to be Joe's. It was his idea, for instance, to put the broken bottles under Mr. Tatlock's car tires, and to dig up the leeks in Albert Finch's allotment. We went along with Joe, but by the time that autumn came, some of his plans were starting to trouble us all.

One evening, when the sky was glowing red over St. Patrick's steeple, and when it was obvious that none of us had anything new to suggest, Joe rubbed his hands together and grinned. He had a rolled-up newspaper stuck into his jeans pocket.

"It's a cold night, lads," he said. "How about a bit of a blaze to warm us up?"

"A blaze?" said Tonto.

"Aye." Joe winked. He rattled a box of matches. "Follow me."

He led us up Swards Road and across The Drive and into the narrow lane behind Sycamore Grove. We stopped in the near darkness under a great overgrown privet hedge. Joe told us to be quiet and to gather close.

"Just look at the state of this," he whispered.

He put his hand up into the foliage and shook it. Dust and litter and old dead leaves fell out of it. I scratched at something crawling in my hair.

"Would *your* dads let *your* hedge get into a mess like this?" he said.

"No," we answered.

"No. It's just like he is. Crazy and stupid and wild."

"Like who?" whispered Frank.

"Like him inside!" said Joe. "Like Useless Eustace!"

Mr. Eustace. He lived in the house beyond the hedge. No family, hardly any pals. He'd been a teacher for a while but he'd given up. Now he spent most of his time stuck inside, writing poems, reading books, listening to weird music.

"We're gonna burn it down," said Joe.

"Eh?" I said.

"The hedge. Burn it down, teach him a lesson."

The hedge loomed above us against the darkening sky.

"Why?"

Joe sighed. "Cos it's a mess and cos we're the Bad Lads. And he deserves it."

He unrolled the newspaper and started shoving pages into the hedge. He handed pages to us as well. "Stuff them low down," he said, "so it'll catch better."

I held back. I imagined the roar of the flames, the belching smoke. "I don't think we should," I found myself saying.

The other lads watched as Joe grabbed my collar and glared into my eyes.

"You think too much," he whispered. "You're a Bad Lad. So *be* a Bad Lad."

He finished shoving the paper in. He got the matches out. "Anyway," he said, "he was a bloody conchie, wasn't he?"

"That was ages back. He was only doing what he believed in."

"He was a coward and a conchie. And like me dad says, once a conchie . . ."

"Don't do it, Joe."

"You gonna be a conchie too?" he said. "Are you?" He looked at all of us. "Are *any* of you going to be conchies?"

"No," we said.

"Good lads." He put his arm round my shoulder. "Blame me," he whispered. "I'm the leader. You're only following instructions. So do it."

I hated myself, but I shoved my bit of crumpled paper into the hedge with the rest of them.

Conchie. The story came from before any of us were born. Mr. Eustace wouldn't fight in the Second World War. He was against all war; he couldn't attack his fellow man. He was a conscientious objector. When my dad and the other lads' dads went off to risk their lives fighting the Germans and the Japanese, Mr. Eustace was sent to jail, then let out to work on a farm in Durham.

He'd suffered then; he'd suffered since. My dad said he'd been a decent bloke, but turning conchie had ruined his life. He'd never find peace. He should have left this place and started a new life somewhere else, but he never did.

Joe lit a match and held it to the paper. Flames flickered. They started rising fast. Tonto was already backing away down the lane; Fred and Frank were giggling; Dan had disappeared. I cursed. For a moment, I couldn't move. Then we were all away, running hunched over through the shadows, and the hedge was roaring behind us. By the time we were back at Swards Road, there was a great orange glow over Sycamore Grove, and smoke was belching up toward the stars.

"Now that," said Joe, "is what I call a proper Bad Lads stunt!"

And no matter what we thought inside, all of us shivered with the thrill of it.

Next morning I went back to the lane. It was black and soaking wet from the ash and the hosepipes. The hedge was just a few black twisted stems. Mr. Eustace was in the garden talking to a policeman. He kept shrugging, shaking his head. He caught my eye and I wanted to yell out, "You're useless! What did you expect? You should have started a new life somewhere else!"

Joe was nowhere in sight but Fred and Frank were grinning from farther down the lane. Neighbors were out, muttering and whispering. None of them suspected anything, of course. They knew us. We were Felling lads. There was no badness in us. Not really.

That was the week Klaus Vogel arrived. He was a scrawny little kid from East Germany. The tale was that his dad was a famous singer who'd been hauled off to a prison camp somewhere in Russia. The mother had disappeared—shot, more than likely, people said. The kid had been smuggled out in the boot of a car. Nobody knew the full truth, said my dad, not when it had happened so far away and in countries like that. Just be happy we lived in a place like this where we could go about as we pleased.

Klaus stayed in the priest's house next to St. Patrick's and joined our school, St. John's. He didn't have a word of English, but he was bright and he learned fast. Within a few days he could speak a few English words in a weird Geordie-German accent. Soon he was even writing a few words in English.

We looked at his book one break.

"How the hell do you *do* it?" asked Dan.

Klaus raised his hands. He didn't know how to explain. "I just . . ." he began, and he scribbled hard and fast. "Like so," he said.

We saw jagged English words mingled with what had to be German.

"What is it?" said Tonto.

"Is story of my *vater*. My father. It must be . . ." Klaus frowned into the air, seeking the word.

"Must be *told*," I said.

"*Danke.* Thank you." He nodded and his eyes widened. "It must be told. *Ja!* Aye!"

And we all laughed at the way he used the Tyneside word.

After school Klaus talked with his feet. Overhead kicks, sudden body swerves, curling free kicks: the kind of football we could only dream of. He was tiny, clever, tough. We gasped in admiration. When he played, he lost himself in the game, and all his troubles seemed to fall away.

"What'll we call you?" asked Frank.

Klaus frowned. "Klaus Vogel," he said.

"No. Your football name. I'm Pelé. You are . . ."

Klaus pondered. He glanced around, as if to check who was listening. "Müller," he murmured. "*Ja!* Gerd Müller!"

Then he grinned, twisted, dodged a tackle, swerved the ball into the corner of the invisible net, and waved to the invisible crowd. All the lads yelled, "Yeah! Well done, Müller!"

The first time Klaus Vogel met Joe was a few weeks after he'd arrived. Since the hedge-burning, things had gone quiet. Joe spent most of his time with Teresa Doyle. We'd seen him a couple of times, leaning against a fence on Swards Road watching us play, but he hadn't come across. Now here he was, strolling onto the field in the icy November dusk. I moved to Klaus's side.

"He's called Joe," I whispered. "He's OK."

"So this is the famous Klaus Vogel," said Joe.

Klaus shrugged. Joe smiled.

"And your dad's the famous singer, eh? The *op-era* singer."

"Aye."

"Giz a song, then."

"What?" said Klaus.

"He must've taught you, eh? And we like a bit of op-era here, don't we, lads? Go on, giz a song." Joe demonstrated. He opened his mouth wide and stretched his hand out like he was singing to an audience. "Go on. You're in a free country now, you know. Sing up!"

Klaus stared at him. I wanted to say, "Don't do it," but Klaus had stepped away, closer to Joe. He took a deep breath and started to sing. His voice rang out across the field. It was weird, like the music that drifted from Mr. Eustace's house. We heard the loveliness in it. How could he *do* such things?

But Joe was bent over, struggling with laughter, and then he was waving his hands to bring Klaus to a halt.

Klaus stopped, stared again. "You do not like?" he asked.

Joe wiped the tears of laughter from his eyes. "Aye, aye," he said. "It's brilliant, son."

Then Joe opened his own mouth and started singing, a wobbly high-pitched imitation of Klaus. He looked at us and we all started to laugh with him.

"Mebbe we're just not ready for it, eh, lads?"

"Mebbe we're not," muttered Frank, turning his eyes away.

Klaus looked at us too. Then he just shrugged again. "So. I will go home," he said.

"No," said Joe. "You can't."

"Can't?"

"We can't let you." He grinned. He winked. "We got to initiate him, haven't we, lads? We got to make him one of the Bad Lads." He showed his teeth like he was a great beast, then he smiled. "'Specially when you consider where he comes from, eh?"

"What you mean?" asked Klaus.

"From *Germany,*" said Joe. "Not so long ago we'd have been wanting to kill you. You'd've been wanting to kill us."

He raised his hand like he had a gun in it and pointed it at Klaus. He pulled an imaginary trigger. Then he smiled. "It's nowt, son," he said. "Just some carry-on. What'll it be, lads? Knocky nine door in Balaclava Street? Jumping through hedges in Coldwell Park Drive?"

"The hedges," I said. I put my hand on Klaus's

shoulder. "It's OK," I whispered. "We're just messing about. And it's on your way home."

So Klaus came with us. We cut through the lanes to Coldwell Park Drive and slipped into the gardens behind, then Joe led us and we charged over the back lawns and through the hedges while dogs howled and people yelled at us to cut it out. We streamed out, giggling, onto Felling Bank. Joe held us in a quick huddle and said it was just like the old days. He put his arm round Klaus.

"Ha!" he said. "You're a proper Bad Lad now, Herr Vogel. You're one of us!"

Then we started running our separate ways through the shadows.

Klaus caught my arm. "Why?" he said.

"Why what?"

"Why we do *that*? Why we do what Joe says?"

"It's not like that," I said. I paused. "It's . . ." But my voice felt all caught up inside me, like it couldn't find words.

"Is *what*?" said Klaus.

He held me like he really wanted to understand. But I had no answers. Klaus shrugged his shoulders, shook his head, walked away.

*   *   *

Klaus kept away from the Bad Lads for a while. He scribbled in his book, writing his story. He sang out loud in music lessons. He dazzled everyone with his football skills during games. There were rumors that the body of his mother had turned up. The whole school prayed for the liberation of East Germany, for the conversion of Russia, for Klaus Vogel and his family.

One day after school I came upon him walking under the trees on Watermill Lane. He walked quickly, swinging his arms, singing softly.

"Klaus!" I said. "What you doing?"

"I am being free!" he said. "My father said that one day I would walk as a free man. I would walk and sing and show the world that I am free. So I do it. Look!"

He strode in circles, swinging his arms again.

"Do I look like I am free?" he said.

"Yes." I laughed. "Of course you do."

He laughed too. "Ha! As I walk, I think of him in his cell. I think of her."

"They would be proud of you," I said.

"Would they?"

"Yes."

He laughed again, a bitter laugh. "And as I walk,

I think of my friends here," he said. "I think of you;
I think of Joe."

"Of Joe?"

"*Ja!* Him!"

"You think too much, Klaus. Come and play
football, will you? Come and be Gerd Müller."

And he sighed and shrugged. OK.

It was getting dark. Frost already glistened on the field.
The stars were like a field of vivid frost above. Klaus
played with more brilliance and passion than ever. We
watched him in wonder. He ran with the ball at his
feet; he flicked it into the goal; he leapt with joy; he
danced to the crowd.

Then Joe was there, his footsteps crackling across
the grass. He had a small rucksack on his back.

"Herr Vogel," he said. "Nice to see you again."

He stepped closer and put his arm round Klaus's
shoulder. "Sorry to hear about . . ." He held up his
hand, as if to restrain his own words. "Our thoughts
are with you, son."

He turned to the rest of us. "Now, lads. It's a fine
night for a Bad Lads stunt."

You could tell it was almost over with us and Joe.

We gathered around him reluctantly; our smiles were forced when he told us he had the perfect trick. But he was tall and strong. He smelt of aftershave; he wore a black Ben Sherman, black jeans, black Chelsea boots. We hadn't broken free of him. He drew us into a huddle. He smiled and told us we'd always been the Bad Lads and we'd keep on being the Bad Lads, wouldn't we?

No one said no. No one objected when he told us to follow. I think I hesitated for a moment, but Klaus came to my side and whispered, "You will not go? But you must. We must all follow our leader, mustn't we?"

And Klaus stepped ahead, and I followed.

Joe led us to The Drive, toward the lane behind Sycamore Grove.

"Not again," I sighed.

"It's like me dad says," said Joe. "He should've been drove out years back." He turned to Klaus. "It's local stuff, son. Probably your lot had better ways of dealing with the Eustaces than we ever had."

Klaus just shrugged.

"Anyway, lads. It's just a bit of fun this time." He opened his rucksack, took out a box of eggs. "Here, one each. Hit a window for a hundred points."

A couple of the lads giggled. They took their eggs. Joe held the box out to me. I hesitated. Klaus took one and looked at me. So I took an egg and held it in my hand.

Joe smiled and patted Klaus's shoulder. "Good Bad Lad, Herr Vogel," he murmured.

Klaus laughed his bitter laugh again. *"Nein,"* he said. "I am not a good Bad Lad. I am Klaus Vogel."

He stepped toward Joe.

"No, Klaus," I muttered. I tried to hold him back but he stepped right up to Joe.

"I do not like you," he said. "I do not like the things you make others do."

"Oh! You *do not like*?" said Joe.

"Nein."

Joe laughed. He mocked the word—*"Nein! Nein! Nein!"*—as he stamped the earth and gave a Nazi salute. He grabbed Klaus by the collar, but Klaus didn't recoil.

"You could crush me in a moment," he said. "But I am not . . . *ängstlich*."

"Frightened," I said.

"Ja! I am not frightened. *Ich bin frei!"*

"Ha! *Frei. Frei.*"

"He is free," I said. And in that moment, I knew that he *was* free, despite his father's imprisonment, despite his mother's death, despite Joe's fist gripping his collar. He had said no. He was free.

Joe snarled and drew his fist back. I found myself reaching out. I caught the fist in midair.

"No," I said. "You can't do that."

"What?"

"I said no!"

Joe thumped us both that night, in the lane behind Mr. Eustace's house. We fought back, but he was tall and strong and there was little we could do against his savagery. Tonto and the others had disappeared. Afterward I walked home with Klaus through the frosty starlit night. We were sore and we had blood on our faces, but soon we were swinging our arms.

"Do I look like I am free?" I said.

Klaus laughed. *"Ja!* Yes! Aye!"

And he began to sing and I tried to join in.

A couple of days later he came with me to Mr. Eustace's house. I knocked at the door and Mr. Eustace opened it.

"I burned down your hedge," I said.

He peered at me. "Did you now?" he said.

I chewed my lips. Music was playing. Beyond Mr. Eustace the hallway was lined with books.

"I'm sorry," I said. "I was wrong."

"Yes, you were."

I felt so clumsy, so stupid.

"This is Klaus Vogel," I said. "He is a writer, a footballer, a singer."

"Then he is a civilized man. Perhaps you can learn from him."

I nodded. I was about to turn and lead Klaus away, but Mr. Eustace said, "Why don't you come inside?"

We followed him in. There were books everywhere. In the living room was an open notebook on a desk with an uncapped fountain pen lying upon it. The writing in the book was in the shape of poetry.

Mr. Eustace stood at the window and indicated the ruined hedge outside. "Is that how you wish the world to be?" he asked me.

"No," I answered.

"No."

He made us tea. There were fig rolls and little cakes. He spoke a few words to Klaus in German, and Klaus gasped with pleasure. Then Mr. Eustace put another record on. Opera. High sweet voices flowing together and filling the house with their sound.

"Mozart!" said Klaus.

"Yes."

Klaus joined in. His voice rang out. Mr. Eustace closed his eyes and smiled.

Me as a kid on the new council estate